DEAD WEIGHT

DEAD WEIGHT

ADDISON SIMMONS

COACHWHIP PUBLICATIONS
Greenville, Ohio

Dead Weight, by Addison Simmons
© 2018 Coachwhip Publications

Addison Simmons (1902-1972)
Published 1946.
No claims made on public domain material.
Introduction © Curtis Evans
Cover: Soda jerk (Library of Congress)

CoachwhipBooks.com

ISBN 1-61646-456-9
ISBN-13 978-1-61646-456-1

INTRODUCTION

ORIGINAL DUSTJACKET FOR
DEATH ON THE CAMPUS

ANOTHER PLAYER IN THE MYSTERY BAND:
The Crime Fiction of Addison Simmons

CURTIS EVANS

The contribution of Addison Simmons (1902-1972) to detective fiction is scanty, consisting, evidently, of but two mystery titles, which were separated by more than a decade: *Death on the Campus* (1935) and *Dead Weight* (1946). Yet beyond his being the author of a pair of detective novels, "Ad," as Simmons was known to his friends, was a prolific professional writer of both short stories and radio plays and a talented musician who as a student at Harvard served as the second director of the University Band. Like his vastly more famous contemporary John Dickson Carr (1906-1977) and such other recently reprinted mystery writers of merit as Todd Downing (1902-1974), Clifford Orr (1899-1951), Evelyn Page (1902-1977) and Dorothy Blair (1903-1976), Ad Simmons is representative of a group of bright, young American college men and women from the Jazz Age for whom a fondness for detective fiction in its bountiful Golden Era (the period, roughly, between the two world wars) served as an entrée—often short-lived, to be sure—into novel writing. Only recently, with the revival of interest in vintage mystery, have we really begun to appreciate the extent of the entertaining legacy left us by these young detective fiction enthusiasts of eighty or ninety years ago, many of whom played but briefly in the mystery band and only now are being rediscovered.

Ad Simmons was born Adolph Sylvan Simmons (Ad seems to have changed his name to Addison while a student at Harvard) in Boston on April 9, 1902, to Jacob and Dora Kramer Simmons,

Russian Jews from partitioned Poland who migrated to the United States in the 1890s. The proprietor of a barbershop, Jacob quickly prospered in the United States. By 1910 he and Dora, a milliner, had moved with their four children—Adolph and two additional sons, Arthur Max and Eliot Daniel, as well as a daughter, Rosalie—into one floor of a recently completed triple-decker apartment house at 128 King Street in Dorchester. (Between 1870 and 1920 over 15,000 thousand triple-decker apartment houses were erected in Boston, particularly in such "streetcar suburbs" as Dorchester, Roxbury, Mattapan, and Jamaica Plain, where as an alternative to tenement and row housing they proved quite popular with the city's emerging middle class.) Jacob passed away at the age of 50 in 1921, but in the 'Twenties Ad attended Harvard University and Harvard Law School and his elder brother, Arthur, Tufts University and Tufts University School of Medicine. While Arthur became a physician, however, Ad, blessed—or cursed as some would see it—with artistic temperament, followed a different and more precarious career path, as did his younger brother, Eliot, who played in an orchestra, and his sister, Rosalie, who graced the stage as a dancer.

Ad quickly evinced wayward artistic tendencies at Harvard, seemingly spending most of his time there immersed in music. Not only did he serve as the college's band director, he wrote his own compositions, such as "Harvard's Own March," and formed his own jazz orchestra, which he dubbed "Addison Simmons' Collegians." The Harvard Band and the Collegians accepted engagements at events around New England, including, for example, the Collegians in 1926 at the Radcliffe Catholic Club's annual dance and the Band in 1923 at the annual Worcester, Massachusetts, concert and dance held at the Hotel Bancroft under the auspices of the Worcester Harvard Club. At the latter affair the band's program included John Philip Sousa's *El Capitan*, Camille Saint-Saens' *The Swan*, Edvard Grieg's Triumphal March from *Sigurd Jorsalfar*, and the Finale of Pyotr Ilyich Tchaikovsky's Symphony No. 4.[1]

In his press publicity as an author in the 1930s, Ad later stated that he had "'fathered' the University Band, in its formative period after the War," which seems a fair enough claim. An advocate of formation marching, which enjoyed a surge of popularity with college and high school bands after the First World War, Ad in a letter to the *Harvard Crimson* defended what he termed "the practice of performing maneuvers" against traditionalists who denounced this practice as mere "gyrations." "The very fact that college bands throughout the country have copied our maneuvers shows how favorably they have been considered in sections of the country outside of our own little eastern cozy-corner," Ad countered. "May I venture to add that some of these bands are among the finest in the country?"[2]

Upon his graduation from Harvard, Ad traveled to Europe for "study," like John Dickson Carr spending considerable time in London and Paris, where he learned jiu-jitsu and organized a dance orchestra which performed at Ostend, Belgium and London's Four Hundred Club ("the most amusing place," confided *The Gourmet's Guide to London*, "to keep awake after all the restaurants are shut"). After returning to the United States he finally got around to attending law school, from which he graduated in 1928. Upon his graduation, however, he asked himself "Who wants to be a lawyer?" and embarked instead upon a career in fiction writing. By 1934, when at the age of 32 he wed Berenice "Bunny" Levin—the pretty, button-black-eyed, 24-year-old youngest child of Sam Levin, a prosperous Fall River, Massachusetts, grocer of Lithuanian origin—Ad had published short stories in the prominent Canadian magazine *Maclean's*. After their marriage the couple settled in Brookline, a town adjacent to Boston where the Kennedy family had resided in the 1910s and 1920s, and Ad began writing his first detective novel, *Death on the Campus*. The next year publisher Thomas Y. Crowell of New York published *Death on the Campus*, along with another mystery which has been reissued by Coachwhip, New Hampshire native Kenneth Whipple's *The Fires at Fitch's Folly*. Ad dedicated the novel to his wife, mother, and brother Arthur.

When Bunny Levin Simmons was growing up, the Levins of Fall River had resided at 298 Third Street, a mere stroll of two minutes from the house where Andrew and Abby Borden, father and stepmother of Lizzie and Emma Borden, were bloodily and infamously murdered with a hatchet on August 4, 1892. At the time when the Levins lived at 298 Third Street, Lizzie Borden of "forty whacks" infamy, who had been tried and acquitted of the horrific murders, lived about a mile away at a much more fashionable home, Maplecroft, where she died in 1927, when Bunny Levin was 17. Among Bunny's siblings at 298 Third Street was Isadore "Izzy" Levin, a rising young lawyer who at the time of Ad and Bunny's nuptials had already argued a case of corporate law before the United States Supreme Court, to the approbation of Justice Louis Brandeis, who approvingly wrote future Supreme Court Justice Felix Frankfurter that Isadore had "made a most creditable appearance in our Court—well prepared, dignified, tactful. With experience added, he should do much."

THE LEVIN FAMILY HOME IN FALL RIVER, MASSACHUSETTS
(PHOTO BY CURT EVANS)

Although I have found no word from Justice Brandies concerning Ad's *Death on the Campus* (we know that near the end of his life Oliver Wendell Holmes, Jr. praised Rex Stout's 1934 detective novel *Fer de Lance*, in which the famous sleuthing team of Nero Wolfe and Archie Goodwin made its debut), the novel was greeted with favorable notices in American newspapers. One particularly creative reviewer, Paul Allen of the *Brooklyn Daily Eagle*, gave his favorable account of the novel in an eight-stanza poem, in a column titled "The Verse Side of Crime":

> Professor Ingram, on his way
> To Chatham House one fatal day,
> Saw things that were a bit askew—
> More so, indeed, than then he knew;
>   Since English was his specialty,
>   He hadn't studied mystery.
>
> So when a chap he'd had in class
> From Chatham House was seen to pass,
> Ben Ingram's subtle mind was not
> Attuned to guess a murder plot;
>   And placidly he kept his route,
>   Not knowing there was death about.
>
> Inside and on his desk Ben found
> A note, as he was fussing round;
> It read: "Come up when you arrive,"
> (Signed) "Yerkes," who then was not alive;
>   For someone else had called on Yerkes
>   And then had given him the works.
>
> It certainly made Ingram hot
> To find his friend completely shot!
> No more would Yerkes and Ingram romp
> In pleasant fields of English comp;
>   And not a doubt existed that
>   The killer was a dirty rat.

Then Ingram called up Prexy Meade,
Who found him upset, indeed,
To realize some bungling fool
Had killed a man right in his school:
    "Ye gods, what will the people say!"
    This thought drove him almost distrait.

Policemen came and found that they
Were not considered quite *au fait*,
For Prexy Meade kept telling how
The news must not be published now;
    And Ingram knowing more than less,
    Just let the bluecoats guess and guess.

Two members of the faculty
He'd seen slink off from tree to tree;
He'd mentioned neither act nor name,
For one was daddy of his flame—
    And in the end he simply had
    To solve the crime to save her dad.

This tale we highly recommend,
It's sure to hold you to the end.
And though it springs a sharp surprise,
"Why not?" you'll say; "It satisfies."

Literally more prosaically, Isaac Anderson of the *New York Times Book Review* pronounced that *Death on the Campus* had "excitement and bafflement galore," while Dorothy Barnes of the Austin *Daily Texan* assured her readers that they would find themselves reading the book at one sitting "because you will be curious enough to ascertain your deductions concerning the identity of the murderer." Particularly amusing is the notice of the novel in the *LA Times,* wherein the reviewer declares that Ad's mystery is "fast enough for any fan," adding: "From the moment Prof. Ingram . . . finds the dead body of Prof. Yerkes, one terror follows rapidly on the heels of another. . . . if you ever thought that college professors are slow and timid, you'll be converted to a new idea."

My copy of *Death on the Campus* is inscribed by Ad to his "good friends and staunch supporters," Bertha and Nettie Trustman, the unmarried daughters of Boston dentist Israel Trustman and his wife Pessie Rubin, who, like Ad and Bunny's parents, were immigrant Russian Jews. The Trustmans settled in the Boston's West End at 59 Chambers Street, making them immediate neighbors of the late actor Leonard Nimoy, whose family lived in a tenement at 87 Chambers Street. Formerly a schoolteacher, Nettie by the time of the publication of *Death on the Campus* had become, according to her nephew, attorney and film screenwriter Alan Trustman (among his credits are *The Thomas Crowne Affair*,

For my good friends
and staunch supporters
Bertha Trustman
and
Nettie Trustman.
Ad Simmons
Boston
January 1936

INSCRIPTION BY ADDISON SIMMONS
(CURT EVANS COLLECTION)

They Call Me Mr. Tibbs!, and *Bullitt*), secretary to the Brookline chief of police "and the only Jew working in the Town Hall."

Not long after the publication of *Death on the Campus*, Ad and Bunny left Brookline for Hollywood, where Ad scripted radio plays for *Hollywood Hotel* and the screenplay for its 1937 film musical version (working with Wyllis Cooper, creator of *Lights Out* and *Quiet, Please*), and later Chicago, where he worked on *The First Nighter Program* and *Grand Hotel,* both of which were sponsored by The Campana Company, a large cosmetics business head-quartered in Batavia, Illinois, and *The Wayside Theater,* sponsored by the Chicago Motor Club. Among Ad's many radio scripts are a number which most definitely are of the crime and mystery genre, including *Dark Dilemma, Three Who Face Death, Bullets in the Night, The Desperate Remedy, Men Don't So Such Things, Six Months to Live, In the Dark, In the Jury's Hands, One Night at the Black Dog* and *Vengeance is Mine* (apologies to Mickey Spillane). The description of *Dark Dilemma* in the *Daily Iowan's* "Tuning In" column suggests that Ad had not forgotten his family's im-migrant origins:

> *The original story centers around co-stars Barbara Luddy, as the girl accused of murdering her vindictive stepfather, and Les Tremayne, as the bum who aban-dons his freight train touring long enough to discover the murder and the murderer. A strong supporting role is played by Michael Romano as Stilette, Les' Italian hobo companion.*[3]

Ad drew on his experience writing for radio when in 1946 he published his second and final detective novel, *Dead Weight*, which was published by Phoenix Press. More than a decade had elapsed since the publication of his last mystery novel, and Ad's writing style had significantly changed since then, becoming much more individualized. *Death on the Campus* was very much a first mystery novel, playing it safe with more of a by the numbers approach (aside from the extravagant dénouement), while *Dead Weight* was exuberant and snappy in writing style and baroque in plot, throwing in, as the *Saturday Review* put it, "everything but sound effects." In the *San Francisco Chronicle* Anthony Boucher for his part pronounced that the novel had "quite a bit of ingenuity."

One might have thought this sufficient encouragement for the 44-year-old author to continue penning crime novels, but perhaps the radio biz, a demanding mistress, sapped Ad's energy for other creative writing efforts. Ad Simmons died in 1972 at the age of 70, apparently without having published another novel in his last 25 years of life. An exploration of his radio mysteries might bear some further interesting fruit for vintage crime fiction fans, however.

Death on the Campus (1935)

While American mystery writers during the Golden Age of detective fiction seem to have lacked the enthusiasm of their English contemporaries for committing murders at primary schools (though there was Stuart Palmer's *Murder on the Blackboard*, 1932, with that indefatigable schoolteacher and snoop

Giving the go-ahead signal in "Hollywood Hotel's" control-room are (left to right): Addison Simmons, staff writer; Diana Bourbon, associate producer; and F. G. Ibbett, the show's producer and director. Standing in the doorway is Onlooker Maury Wood, formerly of Chicago's WGN direction staff

From *Radio Guide* (Jan. 29, 1938)

Hildegarde Withers), they do seem to have enjoyed bumping off teachers and students in colleges, publishing such puzzlers as, for example, Clifford Orr's *The Dartmouth Murders* (1929), John Stephen Strange's *Murder on the Ten Yard Line* (1931), Milton Propper's *The Student Fraternity Murder*, Whitman Chambers' *The Campanile Murders* (1933), Kathleen Sproul's *Death and the Professors* (1933), Addison Simmons's *Death on the Campus* (1935), Joel Y. Dane's *Murder Cum Laude* (1935), Kurt Steel's *Murder Goes to College* (1936), Timothy Fuller's *Harvard Has a Homicide* (1936), and John Miller's *Murder of a Professor* (1937). Addison Simmons's university setting in his novel remains rather anonymous throughout, although the desperately scandal-averse president is a portrait which people should still recognize, sadly today. The dénouement is unexpectedly and rather fantastically violent, yet keen clue fanciers should discern a pleasing trail of clues to follow though the author's maze of mystery, alongside English professor Ben Ingram, who hopes desperately to exonerate from suspicion of murder noted Shakespeare scholar John Hardwick Bailey, father of his winsome sweetheart, Mary.

To me the greatest weakness in the novel, particularly at a time when the female readership of mysteries was markedly expanding, is its lack of any interesting women characters. Women exist in the novel only as highly idealized wives and sweethearts of rather stolid males, as well as a few nondescript housekeepers and one bad girl type, regrettably glimpsed only fleetingly. Having lived more of life within the intervening decade, Ad would evince a stronger grip on the portrayal of the daughters of Eve in his second mystery.

Dead Weight (1946)

In *Dead Weight*, which Ad Simmons dedicated to his beloved wife Bunny, Chicago radio scripters Ed MacIntyre and Walt Tuttle, authors of the hugely popular serial melodrama *Home Town*, decide to quit the grueling radio biz and settle, along with Ed's wife Binnie, in Walt's own home town of Hamsted (probably located in Massachusetts, not very far from Ad's Boston), where they plan to run a pharmacy. "Maybe the hydrochloric would go away and mind its own business and nobody would have to think about nervous breakdowns lurking around the corner," thinks Ed hopefully of their plan; yet almost immediately after their move to Hamsted Ed and Binnie find themselves plunged into a real life case of murder, when Walt is found shot dead in a stall at the pharmacy, a scrap of paper clutched in his hand and a glass of strawberry ice cream soda overturned before him.

So who whacked Walt at the pharmacy? Could it have been someone from Walt's and Ed's old Chicago life, like histrionic radio account executive Harry Leibowitz, imperious radio sponsor Slade Latimer ("one of the wealthiest men in the country") or Latimer's sexy, hot-blooded daughter Sandra, who still carried—rather fiercely—a torch for Walt? Or could the murderer be a local candidate? What does the town simpleton, the strawberry soda guzzling "Dodo" Brown, know about the crime? And is he really as simple as he appears? Ed and Binnie find themselves trapped in a real-life mystery melodrama as strange as anything Ed and Walt ever concocted for *Home Town*—one that puts them in peril of their own lives! Readers who see in Ed and Binnie portraits of Ad and Bunny may just be on to something, but can they beat the fictional couple to the identity of the murderer?

ENDNOTES

[1] "To Play in Worcester," *Harvard Crimson*, 23 April 1923.

[2] "In Defense of the Band," *Harvard Crimson*, 31 October 1923.

[3] Les Tremayne (1913-2003), who replaced Don Ameche on *The First Nighter Program* in 1936, was one of the most prominent America radio performers.

DEAD WEIGHT

FOR BUNNY

1

THE FIRST BULLET

I

Ed's stomach was growling in Chicago. It had started growling in Hollywood, where a nervous breakdown had asked Ed for the next dance. They had come on to Chicago, where the promise of a life with less tension had been the mirage in the desert. It was little better in Chicago. "May I have the next dance now?" the nervous breakdown would say pretty soon.

There was too much hydrochloric acid in Ed's stomach, and when he wasn't pampering it with amphojel and tribasic calcium phosphate three times a day after meals, he was listening to it growl and feeling the hydrochloric burn like an acetylene torch.

Escape, some kind of escape, any kind of escape. that was what he needed. Good old Walt was somewhere on the East Coast opening up the avenue of escape. Little town of Hamsted—something like that. It sounded too good to be true. It sounded like a sleepy little town, a place in which to have an insignificant little business and relax and not make much money—and maybe the hydrochloric would go away and mind its own business and nobody would have to think about nervous breakdowns lurking around the next corner.

Ed was sitting at his typewriter hammering out Episode Nine of the radio serial, with Walt's outline beside the typewriter, when the door of the study opened and Binnie came in like a gust of wind. She cried exultantly, "Here it is, Toots!" and skimmed a telegram envelope across the room into his snatching hands.

"Walt!" said Ed, and tore out the telegram. It was Walt all right. *Chuck out the amphojel and the tribasic wotyoumaycallit,* the telegram said. *I've got it! Sonny boy, we are going to buy a business that will soothe your little old belly to pieces. We will make ourselves seventy-five bucks a week. Call up Lattimer and tell him to go get himself two other boys. We are done, through, finished. Pack your trunk. I will arrive shortly after this telegram. If Harry Liebowitz weeps, lend a shoulder. Love to Binnie. Walt.*

Ed handed the telegram to Binnie and she sat on his lap and read it. When she was done, she drew a long breath of relief. "I don't know if he means seventy-five a week for each of you," she said, "or seventy-five to split between you, but whichever way it is, please let's give three rousing cheers."

"Right," said Ed, and they both stood up and gave three cheers. The study window looked down on the edge of Lake Michigan at the north end of Chicago, and since the window was open, people in their bathing suits on the sand looked up and gaped.

"Just that crazy radio writer," said one of them, who had been trying for years to sell a radio script to the networks and to private sponsors. "They probably just took up his option for another thirteen weeks."

The phone rang and Ed reached for it and sat down. He might have known. "Harry," he said over his shoulder to Binnie.

"Ed!" Harry blazed, "what's this telegram I just got from Walt? Where is he? What's Hamsted? What does he mean, he bought a business? What does he mean here: 'We're done, through, finished; tell Lattimer to go play pattycake?' What does he mean, Ed? What does he mean, he's getting through?"

Harry was a good egg. Ed didn't like to hurt Harry. "Look, Harry, Hamsted is Walt's home town. Walt's been there for several days. He's just bought a nice quiet little business for us to go into and—"

"What do you mean, bought a nice quiet little business?" Harry screamed. "You *got* a nice quiet little business! All you do is sit up there and roll out radio scripts by the yard, at a thousand a week apiece! Could anything be nicer and quieter than that?"

"Look, Harry, be a good guy and don't play dumb. I told you three months ago that I couldn't stand the gaff much longer."

"What gaff? Why do you *talk* like that?"

"Harry," said Ed, "I've got a stomach—remember? It's killing me. My stomach doesn't like our radio sponsor—"

"Ye gods, for a thousand a week do you have to *like* your sponsor? All right, so don't like him; hate him; spit in his eye, but for God's sake, Ed, sane people don't throw away a job at a thousand dollars a week just because they don't like a sponsor!"

"Harry, I don't like to do this over the phone; but I told you—my doctor says if I don't get peace and quiet and a permanent letdown I'm going to have stomach ulcers first and a nervous breakdown next and then maybe a bed of daisies to wear on my chest."

"So what! So you need a rest! So *take* a rest! Take a vacation. Take a week off—take two weeks—take three weeks! But for God's sake don't throw everything up in the air and leave us in the lurch like this!"

"You won't be left in the lurch. We'll give you a couple of weeks to get somebody else to write the script. We'll even coach them if you want us to—or if Lattimer wants us to."

Harry Liebowitz groaned horribly. "Ed, for the love of Holy Mike, don't *do* this to me! *You* got ulcers *coming?* I got mine right here right now—"

"We aren't doing it to you, Harry. We aren't doing it to anybody. We only want rest and peace and quiet—and there's no rest and peace and quiet where there's a Lattimer or any other sponsor, no matter what his name is."

"Ed, *listen* to me!"

"Harry, you listen to me. Once upon a time—"

"Once upon a time!" Harry cried? "Fairy tales he's going to tell me and I'm dying!"

"This is no fairy tale, brother. Once upon a time I had a stomach as good as the next guy's and a set of nerves twice as good."

"I know, I know," Harry wailed.

"I used to write books and love stories for the magazines. I didn't get rich but I used to eat and my stomach knew what to do with the food. Then I got ignorant and went to Hollywood. One radio sponsor ruined my digestion with his heckling, another nearly drove me bats—to say nothing of movie stars who knew more about writing scripts than I did. So we came to Chicago. Chicago wasn't crazy like Hollywood. We had a nice little idea for a nice quiet little radio serial about a nice quiet little country town and we wouldn't be heckled by anybody. Oh no! So you got us a sponsor—"

"I got you one of the biggest sponsors in the country—"

"Sure. So we wrote our little opus and it turned out to be the top ranking serial on the air. All is well for just that long. *Then* Mr. Lattimer steps in. And now he knows more about writing it than Walt and I do. And for two beautiful years out of our lives we've been fighting with Lattimer—day in, day out. If we do it *this* way, Lattimer wants it that way. If we do it that way, he wants it this way. For two beautiful years. Now we're through, Harry. We've got two weeks to go on this option. I'm ahead two weeks on the scripts. I can quit today, and I'm quitting, and you can tell Lattimer *that* for me!"

"I *love* you!" whispered Binnie, who was, sitting straight up on the edge of a chair.

"Lattimer already knows," Harry moaned. "Walt sent *him* a telegram too. So he tells me to tell you to come down to his office—"

"I don't feel up to it, Harry."

"That's what I told him you'd say; so you know what? He's on his way up to your place right now. Ed, think it over, will you? It ain't right to throw away all that money!"

"Binnie." Ed sat down wearily. "Get me a shot of amphojel, will you, honey? Lattimer's coming up here."

Binnie took the phone out of Ed's hand. "Harry," she said, "if that bullheaded millionaire comes up here to bellow at Ed, I won't let him."

"So don't let him in." Harry was sick. "I'm coming up myself. At least, let *me* in. And save a shot of amphojel for me." He hung up.

That was at twelve noon. Forty-five minutes later the door bell rang.

"Let it ring," said Binnie. It rang furiously for five minutes. Lattimer's car was at the curb outside. Finally Lattimer gave up and went away.

"We won't let Harry in either," said Binnie. "Not till Walt gets back. Let Walt handle his half of the battle if it's going to be the last one."

"It's going to be the last one all right," Ed said, sitting wearily in his armchair. "I wish he'd get here. Hey, poochie! Mike!" The big German shepherd came in from the kitchen and put his black, wet rubber nose under Ed's hand.

"I wonder what kind of business Walt bought," Binnie mused.

"I'll bet it's something you never could guess," Ed said. "Something like a butcher shop or something. You know, I could even go for that, after *this* circus."

"A small town!" Binnie breathed. "That'll be delicious. Peace and quiet. Golly, *think* of it!"

The doorbell rang again a little later. That was Harry Liebowitz. They didn't let him in either.

II

Walt came at six. Walt was six feet tall and as aggressive as a district attorney. Walt thought out the plots and Ed wrote them. Ed couldn't plot, Walt couldn't write. Walt had ideas, Ed could make dialogue out of them. It was a perfect combination. Together they had done some of the best stuff on the major networks. They had shot one Crosley rating after another into the skies.

They heard Wait thunder up the stairs. He never took the elevator when he was excited. Binnie threw open the door and Walt scooped her up and tossed her onto the couch, where she bounced high once and then lay still to listen.

"Get my, wire, kids?"

"Yup," said Ed. "What did we buy—a noodle factory?"

"Nope," said Walt, sitting down, "we bought a drug store."

A silly, immensely pleased grin slowly came over Ed's face. "You dog," he said. "Why did you buy a drug store?"

"You know why he bought a drug store," Binnie supplied. "If you've said it once, you've said it a thousand times when you've been heckled the worst."

"What did I say?" said Ed, as if he didn't know.

"You said you'd like to be a country squire and run the neighborhood drug store and Be A Friend To Man."

"But what do we know about drugs?" Ed demanded.

"It's a cinch," Walt said. "We've got two full-time registered pharmacists. We've got a girl at the soda fountain and we've got a slick young feller who manages the whole thing. What we do is learn how to sell the patent medicines, the dishes, the candy, the hardware and haw to manage the place, and there you are."

"Swell," said Ed. "I'm a happy man. Put away the amphojel, Binnie."

Binnie got dinner and for once Ed was so relaxed and happy that he actually didn't need the amphojel. But then the doorbell rang. It was Harry Leibowitz, account executive; Slade Lattimer, radio sponsor and one of the wealthiest men in the country; and Lattimer's daughter Sandra.

Harry was a little man, kept thin by high pressure and worry over advertising accounts. Lattimer was tall and pompous, unbending and stuffed, red-faced and gray-haired; he scorned the earth he trod on, because it was shared by common people; he carried a big whip in his voice and manner; he paid well for radio programs and he was in the habit of treating all who worked for him as stooges, and a stooge had to be beaten into line.

Then there was his daughter. She was tall, slick as an eel's ear, hard as buttons, and beautiful as a bright Toledo blade. Blonde.

Sandra sat down quietly. There was menace in her quiet. Harry Liebowitz sat down uneasily. Lattimer didn't sit down. "What does this telegram mean?" he asked, taking a crumpled ball of paper out of his pocket and holding it out toward Walt.

Walt took time enough to light his cigarette while Lattimer stood motionless. "Just what it says," Walt answered finally. "We're getting through."

"You can't do it," Lattimer said quietly. When he spoke quietly he was worse than when he shouted.

"Yes, we can," Walt smiled. "Look, Lattimer—let's not have an argument. I've checked with our lawyers. We can quit at the end of thirteen weeks just the same as you can fire us at the end of thirteen weeks."

"I won't let you take this show to any other sponsor," Lattimer said. "I won't let you do it."

"Don't worry. We don't want another sponsor. We don't even want the show. We'll sell it to you—cheap. Fifty thousand dollars."

Fifty thousand couldn't scare Lattimer. He didn't even blink. "What good is it to me without you to write it?" he asked, and this time his glance moved to Ed and then back to Walt.

"You mean you'll miss our magic touch?" Walt inquired without a smile. "Thank you. You're very kind. That's the first compliment you'd paid us in two years."

"That's not true. You know very well I've always appreciated the fact that your radio show boosted the sales of my toothpaste."

"Oh, is that so? I always thought it was your toothpaste that boosted our show."

"I don't intend to argue with you, Tuttle. You're just blackmailing me for more money. All right, I'll give it to you. I'll double what I pay you now."

"You can triple it and throw in all the rice in China and you can still keep it," said Walt. "Thanks just the same."

Lattimer's hard eyes went back to Ed again. "What about you?"

"Walt's the boss," Ed told him. "I want to get through."

"You don't like money, eh?"

"We like money. We've got enough. We also like to live. We're going to a small town and try some of that."

Lattimer knew when a fight was over. "All right," he said. "Harry, stay here and see that these two fools give you all the material for the rest of their thirteen weeks. Get together with my lawyer in the morning and draw up the papers. There'll be a check for fifty thousand waiting in my office. And I want no hitches, understand, Harry?"

"Yes, sir," kowtowed Harry.

"Come on, Sandra." Lattimer stalked to the door.

"You go ahead, Dad," Sandra said, her eyes on Walt. "I've got to talk with Tuttle."

"Oh-oh!" said Binnie under her breath, and squeezed Ed's hand a little. Lattimer went out. Ed and Binnie looked at Walt and Sandra and Harry and then they looked at each other. Two was company; five was too much company.

"Don't go away," said Walt, and he sounded in dead earnest.

"We'll just go into the study with Harry," Ed said, "and start talking about the script."

They went down the hall to the study and closed themselves in, Ed, Binnie and Harry. Harry put out lean pleading hands and begged: "Ed, for God's sake, don't do this to me. I'll get Lattimer to do anything you say if you'll only stay on."

Ed shook his head slowly. "What good would it be even if I did stay? Walt wouldn't stay and that's definite, and without Walt I'm no good. You know that. I can't plot a hoot's worth. All I do is string out Walt's plot in dialogue."

"Okay," said Harry mournfully. "Okay. Let's get together on this, then." He sat down at Ed's desk, pulled a sheaf of folded typewritten sheets out of his pocket and spread them out before him.

"Okay," he began. "Here we got Adventure Number Eight of *Home Town*: The Death of Lily Newcomb. In the little town of Stedham, the little country girl, Lily, is already taken in by the villain, Foss Leonard. We have carefully built up the character of the girl and the villain. The girl is simple, straightforward, lovable. The villain is something else again. He is a lawyer now, but in his past life, which no one knows anything about, he was a newspaper man who was run out of the newspaper business because he was crooked. Well, he is still a rat, and Lily is going to have a baby by him. But he doesn't want to marry Lily, because he has spotted something better. Lily is only a farmer's daughter and what he has spotted better is a rich widow. So what does he do? He murders Lily by strangling her. This is terrific here."

"Okay," Ed put in. "That's as far as you've got it. The rest of it is character study. Remorse gets Foss Leonard by the back of the neck and gradually brings him around to a confession." He pulled open a drawer, took out a batch of papers and put them in front of Harry. "And there's the whole thing; lock, stock, barrel and finis of the adventure. And from that point on, you and Lattimer are on your own and—"

There was the sound of a muffled shot from the direction of the living room. Ed and Harry stopped dead still. Binnie jumped up from the couch and said: "What's that?"

Ed flung open the door and ran down the hall to the living room where they had left Walt and Sandra Lattimer. That door too was closed, and he threw it open with a bang.

"You crazy fools!" he hollered. Behind him, Binnie let out a little scared yip.

For Walt had pinned Sandra to the living room wall by her beautiful throat and one arm. Walt's right hand clutched Sandra's throat; his other hand was clamped on the wrist of her right hand, jamming it against the wall, well above her head. In that very capable hand of Sandra's was a gun, a blue-black automatic pistol. Sandra's eyes were venomous slits. Her lips were drawn back taut, so that her teeth showed.

"For the love of heaven," Ed hollered, "what are you two trying to do?"

Walt let go of Sandra's throat, reached up and took the gun out of the hand that he still held pinned to the wall. He emptied the gun and handed it back to her, "Good-bye, Sandra," he said.

Sandra looked at him sullenly for a moment, rubbing her wrist slowly and then her throat. Then she bent down, picked up her handbag that lay at her feet, walked past Ed, Binnie and Harry without a word or a glance and went out the front door.

"Good grief!" said Binnie. "What were you two trying to do?"

Walt waved a dismissing hand. He was pale and his tie was askew, "You know the old plot," he said. "You-can't-run-out-on-me stuff. Who does she think she is?"

"Good grief!" said Binnie again, and looked at Ed. "I knew you two *wrote* melodrama. I didn't know you did it in real life."

"Forget it," said Walt. "It's just one of those things."

"Sure," said Harry Liebowitz, nervously wringing his hands. "Sure."

The bullet was in the wall. Ed went over and looked at it. Then he went into the bathroom and took a triple dose of amphojel.

2

THE SECOND BULLET

I

Main Street cut straight through the heart of Hamsted. It was a well groomed Main Street, with white-striped parking spaces slanting in toward the sidewalk at forty-five degrees. There were hardware stores and shoe stores, men's and women's clothing stores, two banks, a kiddie shoppe, two bakeries, two supermarkets, two newsstands, and a dozen other necessaries-of-life stores beside the two drug stores.

Of the two drug stores, the Hamsted Pharmacy was by far the more impressive. It was a long-established business but it had kept pace with the times. Its exterior had been recently remodeled in black and chrome in the best of taste. Inside was a warmth of welcome and friendliness in the slender mirrors on its walls and the soft white of its indirect lighting.

Walt pushed open the door and held it open for Binnie and Ed. Binnie saw an elaborate perfume bar done chiefly in gold and was sold down the river. "Get a lawyer and some papers," she said at once. "We'll take it."

There was a beautiful redhead behind the immaculate soda fountain. She flashed a smile at Walt just as a trim little man in a white druggist's coat came out of the back room. He was sixty-odd years old and he looked tired. He was tired enough to sell out a thriving business.

"Hello, Walt." He came up briskly and shook hands with Walt and met Ed and Binnie. His name was Oscar Batchelder. All the people in town called him Uncle Batch.

"Have you got any Chanel Number Five?" Binnie asked anxiously.

The old man smiled. "I believe we still have some," he said. "Carl!"

Carl came out of the back room at a lazy long-legged gait. He was dark, sleek and slender, with too long sideburns. Binnie noted that he had eyes almost too beautiful for a man, dark eyes that appraised her casually yet thoroughly before glancing at Ed and Walt.

"Carl," said Uncle Batch, "do we have any Chanel Number Five left?"

"One bottle," Carl replied, looking steadily at Binnie. "One ounce. Would the lady like it?"

"The lady is going to buy it," Walt said, and then, as Carl started for the perfume bar: "Don't bother. She's going to buy the store along with it."

"Oh," said Carl, and though he smiled, his face darkened faintly nevertheless, "I see."

It was then that the idiot came in. Dragging one leg slightly, he moved up to the soda bar and sat down on a stool. The little black eyes glittered in his big head as he looked about him, and he grinned at some thought of his own.

"Hello, Dodo," smiled the redhead.

Dodo began to laugh in great glee. It was a rapturous glee touched off by the girl's smile.

"What're you gonna have, Dodo?"

Dodo chuckled and gurgled with delight.

"Not gonna have nothin'," he said at last. "Not gonna have nothin'. Um broke. Um dead broke—see?" And he laughed, then abruptly became sober.

Walt nudged Ed. "Buy him a strawberry ice cream soda. You'll have a friend for life."

Ed stepped up to the soda fountain. "Ice cream sodas for everybody," he said. "Strawberry for my friend."

The idiot turned a slow gaze on Ed. "Me? For me? Did you say for me?" Ed nodded. "Oh boy oh boy. Strawberry ice cream soda! Oh boy oh boy!" His face grew redder with joy. He rubbed his hands in glee. A fang-like tooth showed on the right side of his crooked mouth—the left side was toothless. There was ecstasy in his eyes as he watched the needle-like stream of carbonated water hiss into the concoction of strawberry syrup and cream; his eyes widened as a great gob of pink ice cream dropped into the jumbo glass. "Oh boy oh boy!"

Without taking his eyes off the boy, Ed realized that someone else had come into the drug store and was standing behind him. Someone touched his shoulder. It was Walt. Ed turned. Walt was shaking hands with a tall, handsome man, broad-shouldered, and it would seem prematurely gray. He was dressed in comfortable brown tweeds and his blue eyes had a jovial light and there were thread-like wrinkles at the corners of his eyes.

"Ed's my partner; Binnie's his wife," Walt said. "The name is MacIntyre—and look, you two, you'd better behave. This is the local newspaper. This guy has his nose in everything—but I mean everything. Once a week, on Saturdays, he tells all. His name is Paul Hastings, reporter, copywriter—I think he sets type, too—and he owns the paper—such as it is: *The Courier.*"

The tall man shook hands with Ed and Binnie. "I'll put you in the Socials, New Inhabitants. I hear you're buying the drug store, Walt."

"That's right. Ed has a complex. He always wanted to be a doctor. He got to be a writer instead. Now the nearest he can get to medicine is a drug store. Good old Ed."

"And how do you fit in? Did you want to be a doctor too?"

Walt smiled slowly. "No. I just want to be home again. And I'm so used to Ed and Binnie I wanted them around too. Owning a drug store will keep them here. You see, I want to write some books, but I can't write, and Ed can."

Hastings chuckled. "That's a funny situation."

Binnie put a fist on her hip. "Walt Tuttle, then this whole thing was a plot—not to get Ed into the drug store business but keep him handy for writing. That's it, isn't it?"

Walt winked a slow wink at Hastings. "Sure," he said. "We're going to write about this town. There's enough story material here for a dozen books. Right, Paul?"

Hastings nodded and looked at Ed, who wore a placid smile. "Your husband doesn't seem to be riled at the deal," Hastings said to Binnie.

"My husband is hypnotized by this store," Binnie retorted. "Just look at him. You could set fire under him and he wouldn't even know it. Look at the silly grin on his face. In his home town there was a druggist that everybody loved and he wants to get to be like that. Can you imagine everybody loving that foolish grin?"

"You appear to love it," Hastings said.

"Me?" said Binnie. "I'm a sucker."

Dodo had finished his ice cream soda and was drawing air and the last bubbles of creamy carbonation noisily through his straw. He gave Ed a beatific smile, slid off the stool and went out contentedly and without a word.

Two men came in as Dodo went out. One was the lawyer who was to represent Ed and Walt in the transaction, the other was to represent Oscar Batchelder.

"Excuse us," said Walt to Paul Hastings. "We're going to close this deal."

II

The lawyer for Walt and Ed was a tall, slant-eyed man named Absalom Reynolds. He was in his early forties, thinly built, with a loose frame and clothes that hung loosely on it, though not without professional neatness. He was a brown man. The slant eyes were brown, the hair was brown, face and hands were brown from the country sun or the country club sun. Suit, shoes and socks were brown.

The lawyer for Oscar Batchelder was chubby and pink-faced with hair that was thin on top, but groomed so as to cover the bald spot as much as possible. He had a habit of smacking his lips as if he were tasting something. His hands were plump and soft and he wore a big diamond set in yellow gold on the little finger of the left hand. When he talked, he rubbed his hands together, palms flattened one against the other, and now and then the motion became one of washing the hands. His eyes were shrewd, yet no shrewder than those of Reynolds. He was dudishly dressed, or overdressed, with pinstripe trousers meticulously pressed and spats against the fast-approaching fall. A large-link yellow-gold watch chain, with a small pendant rabbit's foot rooted in gold, lay across his rounded stomach. He smoked fat cigars, chewing halfway and smoking the rest simultaneously. His name was Hilliard Wells.

Wells had prepared the figures that showed the condition of the business, Reynolds, who had investigated the soundness of the investment for Walt and Ed, spread Wells' figures on the desk in Oscar Batchelder's back room, and checked them carefully while the others waited and Walt and Ed stood looking over his shoulder.

"Everything seems to be all right," Reynolds said at last, and Oscar Batchelder sighed. Hilliard Wells rubbed his hands together.

"Check ready?" Reynolds asked Walt.

Walt had a certified check made out for the amount of twenty thousand dollars. He took it out of his pocketbook, showed it to Ed, who nodded, and passed it to Hilliard Wells. Wells read it carefully, his eyes shining with pleasure, and passed it to Oscar Batchelder. Oscar Batchelder gave it a brief glance and put it in a long brown wallet. His eyes, as he shook hands with Ed and Walt and Binnie, were tired but a little moist with emotion.

"I've been here thirty-five years," he said. "I'm going to get some rest now." He handed Walt two sets of keys to the store. Walt gave one set to Ed.

"Let's have a drink all around to seal the bargain," said Binnie with a reckless air. Hilliard Wells looked at here with amused surprise. Binnie winked at Ed. Ed winked at Walt. Walt winked at Reynolds. Reynolds winked at Oscar Batchelder and they all went out to the front of the drug store and sat in a booth and ordered ice cream sodas.

They were still sitting in the booth when nine o'clock struck. Jennie, the redhead, closed the fountain and went home. Carl Benjamin slipped out quietly. The others got ready to go, but Walt lingered behind.

"I'm going to stay here a while, kids, if you don't mind," he said to Ed and Binnie. "I want to sit and stew a little. I like the atmosphere here. I think I've got an idea brewing for that book."

He winked at Ed. Ed grinned. Binnie shrugged. "I might have known you two couldn't give up writing. I'll probably have to run the drug store."

They all went out except Walt, who locked the door behind them. On the sidewalk they said good night all around. The two lawyers got into their cars and drove off. Oscar Batchelder turned down Ed's offer to drive him home.

"I like to walk in the fresh night air," he said, shook hands with Ed again, raised his hat to Binnie, thrust his hands into his topcoat pockets and moved off down the dimly lighted street.

Ed and Binnie got into their car. They were staying in the big house that belonged to Walt, where Walt had been born and raised, and which had been closed all the years he had been away. Ed and Binnie were staying there until they could find a place of their own.

Walt's house was on a short side street six blocks from Main. Ed drove home slowly, enjoying the quiet of the country.

"Happy now?" Binnie asked.

Ed nodded. "I haven't sent my stomach any amphojel or calcium phosphate or even so much as a Tum all day long."

"I know," said Binnie. "I've been watching. Everything under control?"

"Everything is like peaches," said Ed with a little sigh.

It was their first day in Hamsted. They had arrived that afternoon, had got their luggage settled. A Mrs. Kennicott had spent nearly a week getting the house in shape for their arrival. It was a big house, white with green shutters and with a spacious porch that ran around three sides of it. Ed was thinking of cool evenings on that porch, in a deep chair with his feet up on the rail, when Binnie gave a little start, grabbing his arm. A car had just passed.

"Ed! That was Sandra Lattimer!"

"You're nuts! Where?"

"In that car! The car that just passed! I saw her plain as day!"

"It's night," said Ed.

"I tell you, I saw her! She was with somebody—I didn't see who—but it *was* Sandra Lattimer!"

"So what? If she wants to come and hang on Walt's coat tails, that's *his* business, and he can handle her."

"Yes, with one hand on her throat and the other reaching for her gun! What if the next bullet doesn't get as far as the wall behind him?"

"Let's not butt into Walt's business," Ed said. "He doesn't like it."

"I know," said Binnie. "But I hope we know what we're doing."

III

Ed woke up as if someone had stuck a pin in him. He lay quiet, listening. Beside him, Binnie whispered, "What's the matter, Ed?"

"I don't know. Did you hear Walt come in?"

"No. I just woke up this second."

The light in the hall downstairs shot faint glimmers up the stairway into their room. "He isn't in bed yet," Ed said. "That hall light's still going."

"What time is it?"

Ed pushed the rheostat lever on the electric clock at the bedside and the clock face lighted up with a yellow glow. "It's two o'clock." Ed sat up in bed, poked his feet out onto the floor and felt about for his slippers.

"Where are you going?"

"He ought to be in," Ed said.

"Why?" Binnie queried. "Isn't he old enough to stay out till two if he wants?"

"Sure, but . . . I don't know. I just want to know if he's in."

"Put on your bathrobe, dear. That wind's cold."

Ed yawned and pulled on his gray woolen robe. Then he went out into the hall and walked softly down the hall to Walt's bedroom. The door was open. Ed went in. The shade was up, the window closed. A slanting filigree of moonlight lay across the floor and the foot of the bed. Walt was not there.

Ed put a hand into tousled hair and scratched. He went out to the head of the stairs. He called down softly: "Hey, Walt."

He stood and listened. The only sound was the slow sleepy step of the dog Mike, who came out of the bathroom and put his head under Ed's hand and stood listening too. "Walt." No answer. Ed went downstairs, Mike at his heels, and made the rounds of the rooms, dining room, living room, kitchen, pantry, laundry, den. He came out into the hall again and went to the telephone and called the store. No answer.

And now his uneasiness congealed into a sharp sense of fear. A sudden chill went up his spine. He put the receiver back on its hook and went up the stairs three at a time.

"What's the matter, Ed?"

Ed came into the bathroom, panting. "I don't know, but there's no answer from the store, and that's where he's supposed to be. I'm going down and see if anything's wrong."

"But, Ed, he didn't say he was going to stay in the store. Maybe he went somewhere else."

"Maybe, but I'm going down and see."

He dressed hurriedly.

"Want me to go along?" Binnie asked.

"No—you stay here. If there's any funny business with that Lattimer dame, I may say a few things to her that no lady should hear. . . . So long."

He ran downstairs and out the back way to the garage and drove the car out. He took the street turns without caution and pulled up in front of the drug store with a shriek of brakes.

The light was still going at the back of the store. Ed hurried across the sidewalk and tried the door. It was open and he went in. Walt's keys were in the lock on the inside.

For a moment he saw nothing amiss. The soda fountain gleamed. The perfume bar was a quiet gold. Walt wasn't there. At least he wasn't in sight.

"Walt."

Perhaps he was downstairs, prowling in the cellar for no very good reason. There must be many interesting items in the cellar of a drug store. The light in the office was going and the door was open. Down there must be the stairway to the cellar. Ed started down the length of the store.

He came to an abrupt halt beside the last ice cream booth at the rear. And there was Walt. He was asleep in the booth, chest, head and arms sprawled across the table. It was an ungainly sleep.

"Walt!"

Ed shook him by the shoulder. He was dead weight. The hot blood of panic pounded into Ed's head. "Walt! For God's sake, what's the matter, Walt?"

He shoved Walt upright against the back of the booth and then came the certainty that it wasn't Walt at all, but only his shell. Walt was dead. There was a wide, dark stain under his coat. His face was frozen in a little sardonic, amused smile and the unseeing eyes were wide.

Ed let go of him and he slumped forward again onto the table. Ed backed slowly away until he was leaning against the soda fountain. His knees were shaking and there was a horrible choked feeling in his throat.

He whispered: "Walt!" and the tears were coming slowly down his cheeks. "That damned, lousy woman! That damned, lousy Lattimer!" The tears broke in a torrent. "You wait! You just wait! I'll see you get burned for this if it's the last thing I ever do!"

His arm moved back across the soda fountain in a gesture meant to steady him, and his hand swept through a puddle of sticky liquid. Almost involuntarily he turned to see what it was. A jumbo soda glass, which he had not noticed before, lay empty on its side. It was lined with a pink froth, and the puddle on the counter was pink. . . . Strawberry ice cream soda. . . . For no other reason than that, there moved into his stunned mind the image of the idiot boy grinning and mumbling and sucking a pink soda through a straw.

It was then that he saw the piece of paper Walt's hand was clutching. . . .

3
CHICAGO TIE-UP

I

A girl stood at the dark roadside outside of Hamsted and anxiously watched the lights of an approaching car. The car, slowing as the driver saw the girl, came to a stop beside her when she waved her hat in the white lights. The window slid open. In the dashlight the girl could see the man behind the wheel. He was a tall, thin Yankee with a long, hooked nose and gimlet eyes.

"What's the matter, sister? Want a ride?"

"Yes. To the next town, if you're going that far. Or to the nearest railroad station."

The gimlet eyes blinked. A long arm reached out and opened the door of the car. "Hop in. I'll get you some place or other."

The girl got into the car beside the driver and slammed the door shut.

"What's the matter?" the man asked. "Cut your hand?"

"A little, yes. It's nothing." There was a white scarf wrapped around her left hand. The driver grunted and the car moved on down the road. The man stared straight ahead.

"Out kinda late, ain't you, sister?"

"I suppose so."

"What's the matter—lost?" The long nose was pointed at her now.

"Not exactly."

The man made his grunting sound again and was silent for several seconds. Then: "Stranger around here, are you?"

"Yes."

41

There was another brief pause in the conversation. The car made a right turn and sped on down a roadway as dark as the one it had left.

"That your car I passed back there—smacked into a tree?"

"No." Her eyes had been fixed straight ahead. Now she turned to look at him. "Was there a car smashed?"

"Yup. Four-five hundred yards back of where I picked you up. Thought maybe that's where you hurt your hand."

"It wasn't. I cut it on a glass. I was at a party."

"Walk home from the party?"

She was a little impatient now. A spontaneous answer would have showed her impatience, and she couldn't risk losing the ride by a sharp retort. She frowned and said slowly, in a matter of fact way: "I was driving home with someone—a man—and then all of a sudden I thought it would be a good idea to walk the rest of the way."

"Oh—I get it."

At the next crossroad the car turned right again. Dark pines lined the road to the right. To the left a glimmer of moonlight showed flat fields steeped in a low-hanging fog.

"How far is the next town?"

"Not far. Mile or two."

"Is there a railroad station there?"

"Sure. Where do you want a train for?"

"Boston."

"That your home?"

"Yes."

"Hmph. You don't talk Boston. I'd've swore you talked—well—Chicago maybe."

"I've never been in Chicago."

"No? What's your name?"

"Now look," she retorted, her impatience at last getting the best of her, "I don't have to tell you my name and my past history just because you're giving me a ride. And if you want, you can stop the car here and now and let me out."

"Shucks, now don't get mad. We'll be in town in a minute or two."

She slumped sullenly in the seat. He cast a sidewise glance at her. Then he gave strict attention to the road ahead. The car made another turn to the right and abruptly they were in a wide street with houses on both sides. It was only then that the realization came to her that they had moved in a wide circle.

"Look: where do you think you're taking me? We're back in Hamsted." She would have thrown open the car door to get out and away, but he clamped a powerful hand on her wrist and held her in the seat as the car rolled up to the curb before a low white wooden building over whose door shone a light in a blue globe. The globe bore the lettering: "Police."

"You're right, sister," said the man now. "Back in Hamsted is right. This is the police station. Get out."

II

The chief of police leaned his long arms on the desk opposite Dodo Brown and smiled at him placidly. The chief had been working on Dodo for half an hour without success. Dodo had a sullen glazed eye fixed on the chief's hawk nose as if it hypnotized him. The only light in the room was the desk lamp, which was focused full on Dodo.

"Look, Dodo, be a good feller and just tell us the truth and you can go home or anywhere else you want to go."

"I ain't tellin' nuthin'," Dodo said morosely. "Because I don't know nuthin'. I ain't tellin' nuthin' because I don't know nuthin'. You hear me? I ain't tellin' nuthin'—"

"We heard you the first time," the chief said patiently, still smiling. "Look, Dodo, we know you were in the drug store where we found the man dead—"

"I don't know nuthin'. I didn't kill nobody and I don't know nuthin'."

The chief looked past Dodo at Ed MacIntyre, who sat in a desk chair, the chair tilted back against the wall. Ed was white-faced in the shadows. The newspaper man, Paul Hastings, sat in a corner, leaning forward a little and watching closely, elbows on the arms of his chair, hands folded in front of him His hat was tilted on the back of his head and a cigarette hung loosely from the corner of his lip.

The chief's eye was on Dodo again. "We don't say you killed him, Dodo," he went on. "We just know that you were in the drug store tonight—"

"I was in the drug store," Dodo insisted. "I was in the drug store all right and so was everybody else." He turned and stabbed a chewed fingernail over his shoulder at Ed. "Him—he was there. He buys me a—a strawberry ice cream soda, didncha?" His face lost its sullenness for a moment and he grinned briefly at Ed. "He's a friend of mine, he is. You bought me a soda, didncha?"

Ed nodded soberly. "That's right, Dodo."

"That isn't what I mean, Dodo," the chief went on, and the boy's face became sullen again as he turned reluctantly to face the chief once more. "I mean after he bought you the ice cream soda—several hours after."

The boy hung his head and chewed a nail. "I don't know nothin'," he said.

Ed got up from his chair and came forward and put a hand on Dodo's shoulder. He sat on the chief's desk, his back to the chief. "Look, Dodo," he said, "I'm a friend of yours. Will you tell me?"

The boy looked at the chief. "I won't tell *him*," he said.

Ed looked around at the chief, who got up and went to the door, stepped out and closed it behind him.

"Now tell us," Ed said.

"*He's* here." The boy jerked his head in Hastings' direction. Hastings got up and walked over to the boy.

"You know me, Dodo. You know why I'm here. I'm going to put your picture in the paper, so everybody can see."

The boy looked at Ed and a pleased light began to dawn slowly in his eyes.

"Sure," Ed said quietly, "you want everybody to know how important you are, don't you?"

The boy began to nod eagerly now, looking up at Ed. He considered the prospect of his picture in the paper and a giggle escaped him.

"Come on," Ed prompted. "Tell us. Were you in the drug store after I bought you the ice cream soda?"

A new light now burned faintly in Dodo's eyes. It was a crafty light and it grew in intensity as the idea reached the foreground of his mind. His gaze was fixed on Ed. "I'll tell," he said with a little pleasurable smile, "if you'll buy me another strawberry ice cream soda."

"All right," Ed agreed. "I'll buy you the soda. Now tell us."

"Buy me the soda first," the boy bargained.

"I'll buy you two sodas if you'll tell us now. You can trust me."

"All right," said the boy eagerly. "But don't forget—two sodas —strawrberry."

"I won't forget. Now, tell us: you were in the drug store after I bought you the soda, weren't you?"

The big head nodded; the grin showed long teeth.

"How'd you get in, Dodo?"

"Through the door. Don't forget, you said *two* sodas."

"You'll get two. How'd you get in? Was the door open?"

"Sure it was open. It was open a little bit. Like this." With finger and thumb held up before his eye, he indicated an opening of a quarter of an inch, through which he peered now as if looking through the crack in a door ajar.

"And you went in?"

"Sure."

"What time was it when you went in—do you know?"

"Sure I know. I seen the clock in there. It was quarter of two."

"All right, it was quarter of two. Now, did you close the door after you when you went in?"

"Sure. I closed it after me."

"The lights were on in the store, weren't they?"

"Oh, they was on all right."

"What was the first thing you did inside there?"

"I—" He looked nervously from Ed to Hastings and back to Ed. "You ain't gonna be mad at me, are you?"

"No. We won't be mad."

"You're gonna buy me a strawrberry soda—strawrberry *ice* cream soda—*two* of 'em—no matter what?"

"That's right," Ed nodded. "What was the first thing you did inside there?"

The boy grinned sheepishly. "I made me a strawrberry ice cream soda," he confessed.

"You went behind the soda fountain and made yourself a soda—is that right?"

"Yeah. Only you ain't mad, are you?"

"No-no. I'm not mad, Dodo. You just go on now and tell us what else happened."

"Well . . . I drank the soda."

"You spilled some of it, didn't you?"

"Yeah. I knocked the big glass over when I seen—him."

"Just what did you see, Dodo?"

The boy's eyes rolled nervously. He wrung his fingers.

"I didn't do nuthin', mister," he said.

"We know you didn't. All we want to know is what you saw."

"Well . . . I seen *him* there, you know who, sitting in there in the booth and lyin' with his face down right across the table. I didn't see him at first, mister, or I wouldn't of took the ice cream soda—honest to God. I only seen him all of a sudden and I kinda jumped and that's when I knocked over the strawrberry ice cream soda."

"What did you do then, Dodo?"

"Nuthin'. I got scared and ran away."

"Didn't you go over to the table and look at the man who was there?"

"No." The eyes were downcast. He chewed a fingernail.

"Look, Dodo. When they brought you here a little while ago, they put some ink on your fingers and made fingerprints on a piece of paper, didn't they?"

"Sure. Just like they do in the movies. I know. I seen 'em . . . in the movies."

"Then you know what they did it for—right?"

"I guess mebbe so."

Paul Hastings said quietly: "Suppose I told you, Dodo, that they found your fingerprints on the table alongside the man who was lying there?"

The boy's head jerked up. "No they didn't!" he flared. "I wiped 'em up!" And then he realized that he had been trapped and his mouth hung open and his hand went slowly to it and he stared fearfully at Hastings and then at Ed. Hastings smiled and stepped back.

"It's all right, Dodo," Ed said. "Don't be scared. Just tell me what really happened."

The boy gulped and looked down at the floor guiltily. His forehead worked itself into deep wrinkles. Then, in a moment, his lips moved as if he were talking to hint self silently. He sat thus for a full minute, then looked up quickly at Ed without raising his head, then looked down again.

"Tell us what happened, Dodo."

It took half a minute for the question to penetrate the maze of thought that engulfed Dodo's mind. "Nothin' happened," he said without glancing up. "He was dead and there was some blood and I thought I could be a detectif and find out who done it—like they do in the movies."

Ed met Paul Hastings' glance. Hastings' eyebrows were raised and there was a little smile of surprise on his face.

"Oh," Ed said. "You want to be a detective, like you see in the movies." The big head nodded; the eyes were downcast. "Did you find any clues, Dodo?"

Dodo thought for a moment. His feet shuffled on the floor and he twisted his fingers nervously once: more. "No," he said. "I didn't find nuthin'." But from the way he looked up, from the craftiness again in his eyes, Ed judged that he was lying.

"Look, Dodo," he said. "They found a piece of paper in the dead man's fingers. He was holding tight to it with his left hand. It was just the corner of a piece of paper. The rest of it was gone. It was torn off by somebody. Did you tear it off, Dodo?"

"No!" the boy protested. "I didn't do no such thing. I didn't do no such thing at all."

"Did you see anything in his hand at all?"

"No." The tone was leaden, the eyes downcast again.

"Got anything else to tell us, Dodo?"

"I don't know nuthin' else."

"Okay, Dodo. You come down to the store tomorrow and I'll see that you get two ice cream sodas." Ed glanced at Hastings. "If you can drink three, you can have three sodas, Dodo."

The boy's head came up and his face lighted. "Sure! I can drink three! Oh boy! I can drink three all right! Gee—thanks, mister! Thanks!"

III

"What's your name, sister?"

Sullen, cold blue eyes stared at the chief of police, meeting his eyes without wavering, without so much as blinking. The chief leaned forward at his desk. "I asked you, what's your name, sister?"

The girl said coldly: "You haven't any business keeping me here. You had no right to bring me here and you haven't any right to ask me questions. I'm getting out of here."

"Sit right where you are, sister. You aren't goin' any place. You'll tell me your name or I'll lock you up."

"You do and my father'll smash you and the rest of your hick police force into little pieces. You hear me?"

"I hear you. What's your father's name?"

"What right have you got to keep me here? You'd better tell me or I'll—"

"Sure. I'll tell you. You're under arrest on suspicion of murder and—"

The girl jumped to her feet. "Look, you hayseed cop. I don't know what you're talking about. I don't know anything about any murder and I don't know anything about—"

"Know anything about this?" the chief drawled, sitting back and reaching into the right pocket of his suit coat. He took out an envelope that had "Hamsted Police Dept." stamped in one corner and he opened it and took out a triangle of paper with two smooth edges and the third rough where this corner of a sheet of paper had been torn with the rest of the sheet. It was blue gray. It had a thin dark blue border running along the two smooth edges. The girl watched with eyes that first widened and then narrowed once more and tried to appear normal. The chief had his attention fixed on the piece of paper, which he laid before him on the desk. Now he looked up at the girl and motioned to the paper.

"Look," he directed. "Printed right across the top, embossed nice and expensive, it says Sheridan Road. The rest of the address is torn off. And right here is written yesterday's date. Is that your handwriting or isn't it?"

"No, it isn't!" the girl snapped.

The chief thoughtfully passed a long, bony hand over his chin. "You live on Sheridan Road, in Chicago?" he asked.

"No, I don't. I told you I live in Boston and—"

"Sure, I know you did, and it'll be easy to prove, one way or the other. I thought you'd like to save us some time and trouble. But if you won't—" He broke off, and got up by putting his hands on the arms of his chair and pushing himself up a little wearily. "Just a minute." He walked a few steps to a door at the right of the desk and opened it. "Come on in," he said, and stood aside, turning to watch the girl.

Ed MacIntyre came in, followed in leisurely fashion by Paul Hastings. "Hello, Sandra," Ed said.

The girl sat down slowly, as if overcome by sudden fatigue.

"Look," the chief said. "I don't know how you figured you'd get away with it. We know who you are and where you're from and we know you came here and killed Walt Tuttle. Now the quicker you come clean, the better for you."

The girl was trembling now, a barely perceptible tremble. Blood was dark on the white scarf that covered her left hand. The right hand was frozen in a white rigid fist, clenched tight in her lap.

The chief went on: "Miss Lattimer, you sent an air mail letter to Walt Tuttle yesterday from Chicago. Mr. MacIntyre here found it in the mail and gave it to Tuttle. Now do you deny this piece of paper was yours and that you sent it?"

"What if I did?" the girl asked slowly. "That doesn't give you any right to arrest me and tell me you're holding me for murder!"

"Doesn't it? Then maybe you'll explain why you beat it out of town right after Walt was killed and you beat it so hell-bent fast you didn't see the curve in the road there and smashed the car right into a ditch. Maybe you'll tell us why—"

"I don't have to listen to any more of this," Sandra cut in. "I know what my rights are. I want a lawyer and I want my father and I won't say another word till they both get here!"

The chief shrugged. "The lady knows her rights," he admitted. "And I know mine, sister. I'm putting you in a nice comfortable little cell till we get things all arranged nice to your satisfaction. All right, sister, get going." He pressed a button at the corner of his desk. A door behind Sandra opened and a uniformed officer came in. "Bill," said the chief, "put this lady in guest chamber number six. She's gonna be waitin' for company. However, if she decides to talk before company comes, just let me know."

IV

The body had not been moved, pending arrival of the district attorney's men. Now they were there, in the drug store, taking fingerprints from every conceivable spot, taking pictures of the store from every angle and sketching the layout in the preliminary detailed preparation required by a trial for murder.

Henry Depew, assistant district attorney in charge, was standing in front of the soda fountain with Chief Tomlin. Depew was tall and rangy, only an inch shorter than the chief of police. He stood listening to Tomlin's survey of the facts to date, eyes on the floor, hands thrust deep in his trousers pockets, an inch of dead cigar between his teeth. Ed MacIntyre and Paul Hastings, covering for his paper, completed the group.

"MacIntyre here," the chief was saying, "after he phoned from Tuttle's house and didn't get any answer, he came down to the store to see what was keeping Tuttle. He got here about quarter past two. The door was unlocked. He came in and found him there. Then he phoned me and I came right down. I rounded up the man on the beat, Johnny Brewer, and Brewer had this to add: About ten minutes before MacIntyre walked in here, Brewer saw a girl come out. There was a light going in the store, enough light so that he got a pretty good look at her. She got into a car that was parked right in front of the door and drove off like a shot. Brewer doesn't know whether she saw him or not; he was on the other side of the street. Anyway, Brewer got the number of the car, and then a few minutes after *I* got here to the drug store the station house got a report from a truck driver named Malone that he was driving towards Hamsted here when he saw a car try to make the turn at Gordon Road and go right into the ditch. He stopped his truck and went to see what was what. The girl got out of the car just as he came up, and when he spoke to her, she made a beeline down the road, away from him; so he just said 'Nuts' and came into town and reported. I went right out, spotted the smashed car and picked the girl up further down the road and brought her back. She's an old flame of Tuttle's and her old man's a millionaire named Lattimer and she wants her old man and a lawyer before she'll talk."

"Where's her old man?" Depew asked.

"Chicago."

"Anybody got in touch with him yet?"

"Yup. We phoned just before you got here. He's taking the next plane."

"Got a lawyer for her yet?"

"We got Hilliard Wells out of bed."

"The fat boy?"

"If you think he's a boy. He's in a huddle with her now."

Depew chewed his dead cigar during several moments of silence.

"No sign of the gun?"

"Nope. It wasn't in the wrecked car. I took a good look when I drove out to it. 'Course, she could have got rid of it in the bushes anywhere along the road, either before she got wrecked or afterwards."

"Sure. Now what about this town moron of yours?"

The chief looked at Ed. "Tell him what you got, Mr. MacIntyre," he said.

4
ALIBI

I

Assistant District Attorney Depew was no respecter of sleep. He routed out of bed the following persons: Oscar Batchelder; Jenny Sofia, the red-headed soda clerk; and Carl Benjamin. These three he kept closeted in an antechamber two doors down the hall from the chief's office while he worked on Dodo Brown.

But working on Dodo was a fruitless business. He maintained placidly that he had told all that he knew to Ed MacIntyre for the price of three "strawrberry" ice cream sodas, that he knew nothing else to tell and that he was not going to talk with anybody except Mr. MacIntyre about it. Neither the specific threat of a cell downstairs nor suggestion of unnamed worse things that the law had to offer as inducement made any impression on him. He had told all he knew to the only man he would tell it to and except for collecting his *quid pro quo* he was through with the whole matter. He leered at the assistant district attorney with no fear now but with a certain strange self-satisfaction. The madder Depew became, the more self-confident was Dodo Brown. And at last, after progressive wheedling, coaxing, barking and bellowing, Depew tore a comparatively fresh cigar into shreds, hurled them into Chief Tomlin's fireplace and had Johnny Brewer hustle Dodo from the room.

Next in turn, Jenny Sofia knew nothing. She had left the store at closing time. She had had a date with Mike Jaffa. She had met him at the corner of Main and Porter, they had driven a mile out of town to the Roma, where they had had a glass of beer and a couple of dances, after which Mike had driven her home. She had said good night to Mike at midnight, had gone to bed and knew nothing more until Johnny Brewer rang the doorbell and woke her up. The assistant district attorney chewed a fresh cigar and appraised her carefully: Red hair, red lips, red nail polish; peaches and cream complexion; flashing white teeth.

"That's all," Depew said. "You can go." He scowled at Chief Tomlin, who sat at his desk while Depew walked up and down.

Nor did Carl Benjamin know anything. More than anything else, he was disgruntled because his sleep had been disturbed. He was sullen-eyed and his customarily sleek hair was without its lacquer finish. He had gone straight home and to bed; his mother could testify to that. He was sorry that Mr. Tuttle was dead because he was a nice fellow, but he didn't know anything about it.

"You can go too," said the assistant district attorney.

Oscar Batchelder had more to offer. He had gone home to bed, but he had been unable to sleep, so he had dressed again and come wandering downtown. He had been irresistibly drawn to the store that had been his own so recently. A light showing through the drawn curtains had puzzled him; it was so late. He went to the door and knocked. At first there was no answer. He wondered if someone had unwittingly left the lights on and gone home, but then he heard a brief exchange of voices—men's voices—and after that footsteps approached the door. The door opened and it was Walt Tuttle.

"What time was that?" asked Mr. Depew.

"I don't know," replied Oscar Batchelder.

"What! You mean to say you got up in the middle of the night and went for a stroll down the street and you didn't know what time it was?" He glared disbelievingly at Batchelder.

"That's right," said Oscar, nodding his gray tired head in an automatic way.

"What time was it when you got out of bed?"

"I don't know."

"Now, don't give me that, Mr. Batchelder!" said Depew wearily. "When a man wakes up in the middle of the night; he looks at the time instinctively!"

"Does he?" said Mr. Batchelder with great patience. "Well, here's one who doesn't. Now, don't bark at me, Mr. Depew. That won't make me tell you something I don't know. I'm in the habit of waking up at night. I have insomnia—probably from over-work. Time doesn't mean anything to an insomniac."

"I have insomnia too! When *I* wake up, I *always* look at the time first! It's the natural—"

"I used to do that too," Mr. Batchelder cut in quietly. "But when you've had as much insomnia for as long a time as I have, you just get up and go out for a walk without looking at the time. You see?"

"All *right!*" said Mr. Depew. "Suppose we get on with this. Mr. Tuttle opened the door of the drug store. What then?"

"Well, I looked past him just in time to see the door to my office—well, what used to be my office—I saw that door clos-ing slowly, as if someone wanted to close it without making any noise."

"Then what?"

"Mr. Tuttle asked me if I wanted anything. I said no, I didn't want anything and I asked him if everything was all right."

"Why did you ask him that? Did you have any reason to think there was anything that wasn't all right?"

Mr. Batchelder looked vaguely puzzled. "That's funny," he said at length.

"What?"

"Mr. Tuttle asked me the same thing you asked me just now. When I asked him if everything was all right, he wanted to know why: did I have any reason to think there was anything that wasn't all right?"

"What did you tell him?"

"I said no, that I was just asking."

"But you had a feeling that things weren't just right?"

Oscar Batchelder's fingers drew slowly at his lower lip while he stared at the floor. Then he looked up and said: "Yes, I did."

"Why?"

"I don't know. I'm not psychic. Didn't you ever get a feeling that something was wrong and not know why?"

"Yes," retorted Depew sourly. "I've got one now." Batchelder looked at him quizzically and mildly. "Go on. What did you do next?"

"I didn't do anything. I only saw something."

"What? What, man, what? What did you see?"

"A package of tobacco."

"A package of tobacco! What about it?"

Batchelder considered the question carefully. He held a silence of several moments, during which he seemed to be almost oblivious to Depew's presence and to the presence of the stenographer who took down his answers, and to Chief Tomlin too.

Depew, who had been fencing with Oscar Batchelder at ten paces, now marched up and thrust his face down close to the little druggist's.

"Forgive me if I'm boring you," he snapped, "but I just asked you a question."

"Eh?" said Mr. Batchelder, coming momentarily out of his preoccupation. "Oh. Oh, yes. What about the tobacco, you asked me? That was it?"

"That was it. What about it?"

"Nothing," replied Mr. Batchelder quietly. "It was just a package of pipe tobacco: a package of Brewer's Blend. It was on the table of the last booth in the store."

"Proving what?"

"Eh? Oh. Oh, proving it—it wasn't a woman—that's all."

"You mean it wasn't a woman that was there with Mr. Tuttle?"

"That's what I mean."

"It doesn't prove any such thing. How do you know the tobacco wasn't Mr. Tuttle's?"

"Mr. Tuttle didn't smoke a pipe. He smoked only cigarettes. I know because he told me so."

"All right. But how do we know that there weren't two people there with Mr. Tuttle—a man and a woman?"

Mr. Batchelder shrugged. "Maybe that's just who was there."

Mr. Depew glared at him. "Are you trying to confuse the issue, Mr. Batchelder?" he demanded.

"I? No indeed. I'm doing my best to offer any information that might clear the issue."

"All right then, go on."

"There isn't much more. It wasn't any of my business what was going on in the store, so I just excused myself and went out. I walked home and went to bed—and that's all know!'

"Okay," said Mr. Depew, giving up. "You can go."

Mr. Batchelder nodded, got up and walked out slowly. As the door closed behind him, Depew cast a quizzical glance at Chief Tomlin. "Do you see any significance in the package of tobacco?"

The chief scratched his nose, thought about it carefully, then shook his head. "Nope."

"Well, *I* certainly don't," said the assistant district attorney. "Brewer's Blend is a national seller. Anybody in the country could be carrying a package of it. . . . All right, now where do we stand, Tomlin?"

"Right where we stood when we began. The girl did it. He threw her down, and she killed him for it."

The assistant district attorney nodded slowly and began to walk up and down, hands thrust deep in his trousers pockets, his chin on his chest. "I guess so," he said. "Nothing else makes sense. It fits neat as a jigsaw puzzle." He stopped walking. "Except that package of tobacco."

II

Attorney Hilliard Wells emerged from his rendezvous in Sandra Lattimer's cell at seven o'clock in the morning. There was a mildly triumphant smile on his face as he walked through the ante-room outside the chief's office, waved a fat hand at Ed MacIntyre and Paul Hastings and bustled out. He got into his car in front of the building, swung the car around and drove two blocks to a big modern dining car. He ran his car into the driveway, pulled up with a zip of his parking brake and strolled into the diner. He raised a hand in silent reply to the "Hello, Mr. Wells" of the man behind the counter and looked from one end to the other of the long eating room. A beatific smile blossomed on his face as he espied the diner's lone customer, a man in the last booth at the end of the dining car. Mr. Wells looked at the white-capped counter man and nodded his head in the direction of the man in the booth and asked a question with his eyebrows.

"He's been here all night," the counterman said. "He's been sleepin' for hours. *I* never saw him before."

Wells nodded and strolled down the length of the diner. The man at the table was asleep, hunched into the corner of the booth, head against the wall, arms folded across his stomach. He was dark, with a little black mustache and a certain air, even in sleep, of slick sophistication. He was snoring faintly.

Hilliard Wells sat down opposite him, studying his subject placidly for several seconds. Then he cleared his throat and said: "Mr. Liebowitz."

The man stirred a little but did not waken. Mr. Wells reached out with a fat forefinger and poked him in the shoulder.

Mr. Liebowitz wakened with a start. He sat up straight and stared at Mr. Wells through sleep-laden eyes.

"Hello, Mr. Liebowitz."

Briefly Mr. Liebowitz continued to stare, blinking sleep away. He stared suspiciously and yawned at the same time.

"Have you slept well, Mr. Liebowitz?" Wells inquired casually, smiling his friendliest smile.

"I guess so," said Liebowitz. "Who are you?"

Wells clasped fat hands on the table and leaned forward. "My name is Hilliard Wells. I'm attorney for Miss Sandra Lattimer."

Harry Liebowitz' eyes had wandered from Mr. Wells. They returned to him slowly, and their look was puzzled. "What's she want an attorney for?"

"To defend her against a murder charge."

Harry Liebowitz' head snapped up as if he had had an electric shock. "To—*what?*"

"To defend her against a murder charge," Wells repeated soberly.

Liebowitz swallowed with some difficulty. "What do you mean? Who'd she murder?"

Wells opened his clasped hands in a little shrug. "I don't think she murdered anyone. But right now she's under arrest for the murder of one Walter Tuttle."

III

Assistant District Attorney Depew sat at Chief Tomlin's desk. Chief Tomlin sat next to him, and both of them faced Hilliard Wells, who stood leaning forward against the chief's desk, supporting his weight with spread fingers on the desk top. Wells was speaking.

"I take it," he said to Mr. Depew, "that what you're out for is not just an arrest—not just anybody to pin this on—you're out after justice."

Mr. Depew's gaze was sour. "Don't talk like a damned ass! he said. "Of course I'm out after justice! What are you getting at?"

"I'd like to show you," said Wells congenially, rubbing his fat hands together.

"No one's stopping you."

"No, no one's stopping me, but may I have cooperation?"

"What do you want?"

"I want Miss Lattimer brought to this office now—at once. I want to question her in front of you and present to you evidence which otherwise I would have to present in court, much to your embarrassment."

Depew sent a gloomy look in the direction of Tomlin. "Have her brought in," he directed, and Tomlin reached out and buzzed for Johnny Brewer, who poked his head in a moment later.

"Bring in her ladyship," Tomlin said.

"Oke," said Johnny, and closed the door again.

"Thank you," said Hilliard Wells. "I'll be back in a moment." He went out by the door that led to the anteroom and returned presently with Harry Liebowitz and the counterman from the all-night diner.

"Sit down, gentlemen," said Wells.

Liebowitz, hatless, sat down and wiped a moist forehead and twisted his damp handkerchief in nervous fingers, his gaze going back and forth in a peculiar slow worried way from Tomlin to Depew. The counterman, wearing his small white cook's hat, was only bored and tired. His feet hurt and he wanted to undo his shoes.

Johnny Brewer threw open the door and stood aside to let Sandra Lattimer walk in. She came in sullenly, not noticing Harry Liebowitz at first.

Harry jumped to his feet and rushed across the office to her. "For God's sake, Sandra," he cried, "what's this awful mess about? Walt's dead! Do you hear me! Walt Tuttle's dead!"

"I hear you," the girl replied evenly. "I've been hearing some other things, too, the best one of which is that I was the one that killed him." She looked scornfully at the chief and at the assistant district attorney. "You're a couple of nitwits," she said. "I didn't kill him. I was crazy about him."

The assistant district attorney was about to reply to that when Hilliard Wells stepped forward.

"Sit down, Miss Lattimer. Let me handle this. Sit down here." He pulled a chair up to the desk.

The assistant district attorney muttered bitterly, "She was crazy about him," got up and went to the door to the anteroom, opened the door and said, "Mr. MacIntyre, come in here."

Ed MacIntyre, looking more peaked than ever, came in on tired legs. Paul Hastings came to the threshold, looked in and inquired: "How about me? Is the press wanted?"

"Of course the press is wanted," Wells declared. He looked at Depew and rubbed his fat hands together.

"In the interest of fair play. We have no secrets from the public, have we, Mr. Depew?"

"You're welcome to stay, Hastings," Depew said. Then to Ed: "Mr. MacIntyre, this lady has just stated that she didn't kill Walter Tuttle because she was crazy about him. Will you kindly tell her attorney what happened in Chicago because she *was* crazy about him?"

"Yes," Ed nodded. "She tried to shoot him in Chicago because she was crazy about him."

"That's fine," said Depew, turning to Hilliard Wells. "Now suppose you go on from there."

"Certainly," said Wells, clearing his throat. "Now, Mr. Depew, since you state that you don't wish to try an innocent person and that you also wish to cooperate in the interests of justice, will you kindly verify the following facts: One, the body of the victim was discovered by Mr. MacIntyre shortly after two a.m. this morning. That's right, is it not?"

"Yes."

"The medical examiner in his preliminary report stated that Mr. Tuttle had been dead about two hours. That's right too, isn't it?"

"That's right."

"And the medical examiner made his examination at about half past two this morning?"

Depew nodded grudgingly.

"Good!" said Wells cheerfully. "Mr. Tuttle, then, was murdered at about half past twelve. Very well. Now!" Wells turned to face the counterman. "This man, Mr. Depew, is in charge of Rawson's Diner from ten p.m. to eight a.m. His name is Bill Carter. Bill, I'd like to have you answer a few questions for the benefit of the district attorney. At what time did this young lady, Miss Lattimer, and this gentleman, Mr. Liebowitz, come into the diner last night?"

The counterman was lean-jawed and blue-eyed. His jaw moved a little with a cud of chewing gum and his eyes went to Depew. "They came in just after I went on duty, maybe five or ten minutes after ten."

"What did they do when they came in, Bill?"

"Well, first the lady asks me if we've got a phone booth. I showed her the phone down at the end of the diner. It ain't in a booth, but it's a pay station and she went and called somebody up."

"Did you hear anything that she said?"

"Yeah, some. She was talkin' with somebody she called Walt. She wanted to see him right away."

"What else did you hear?"

"Nothin' much, except she said she was there with—I guess the name was Harry, she said—and then she read off the number of the phone there in the diner."

"Then what did she do?"

"Well, she said something about she'd be waiting for a call."

"Anything else?"

"Yes. This gentleman here"—he indicated Harry Liebowitz—"he got up and went over and she gave him the receiver and he began to say something about for God's sake he had to see this Walt fellow tonight and not to let them down—and that was about all, I guess."

"All right, Bill. Now, that was a little after ten. Can you tell us how long Miss Lattimer and Mr. Liebowitz stayed there in the diner?"

"Yes, sir. They were there until five minutes of two. Well, he was there after that; he stayed right through; but she got up and went out at five of two. And she didn't come back."

"How do you know it was five minutes of two when she left?"

"Well, they'd been hanging around so long, I just took a look at the clock to see what time it was when she went, that's all."

"And Mr. Liebowitz stayed on?"

"Yes, sir. He fell asleep in the booth. He was sawin' wood, but good."

"All right, Bill. Now, Miss Lattimer." He turned to face Sandra. "Miss Lattimer, suppose you tell us your version of what happened. Start with your arrival in Hamsted."

"I'll go farther back than that," Sandra began quietly, looking only at Hilliard Wells. "Harry and I flew from Chicago to Boston yesterday afternoon. We rented a car and drove down here to Hamsted and we got here about ten o'clock. We went into the diner for a cup of coffee. Harry wanted to talk to Walt right away, and so did I. We didn't know just where to go, but Harry knew the name of the drug store they'd bought, so I took a chance and called there. Walt was there. I told him I wanted to see him. He asked me where I was and I gave him the phone number of the diner. He said he was busy but he said he'd phone me back when he was free. He said it might be an hour or even

more before he called and I told him I'd wait no matter how long
it was."

"Good," said Wells. "Now just a moment. Mr. Liebowitz."
Harry Liebowitz turned his head quickly; he had been studying
the reactions of Chief Tomlin and the assistant district attorney.
"Mr. Liebowitz, you talked to Mr. Tuttle. Tell us about it."

Harry Liebowitz spread out, empty hands. "There's nothing
to tell," he said. "I simply told Walt that I made a flying trip here
to talk with him about this radio script he used to write. I told
him we had a bunch of God-forsaken halfwit writers in Chicago
that were murdering it cold and I wanted his advice on what to
do. He said he could see me a little later, that he was going to
call Sandra back anyhow, and then we'd get together. That's all."

"Very well. Now, Miss Lattimer again. What did you do from
that point on?"

Sandra's eyes were fixed on the floor. She spoke without looking up. "Well," she began slowly, "Harry and I sat there in the
diner and talked and had something to eat and it got to be late. I
kept thinking I'd better call Walt again—that maybe he'd left the
store, that he'd forgotten to call me back. But, knowing Walt, I
figured it wouldn't do any good to phone again; he was just the
kind that would get sore if I didn't do what he said and refuse to
see me altogether. So I decided just to go and see him—"

The assistant district attorney interrupted quietly. "You didn't
figure at the same time that he'd be sore if you just made your
appearance—unexpectedly after he told you he'd call back?"

Sandra's eyes remained fixed on the floor. "I wanted to see
him face to face; that was different from giving him a chance to
hang up on me."

"Go on."

"I went out and got into the car we had hired and drove to
the drug store."

Depew interrupted again. "Did you know how to get there?"

"No. I just—"

"You didn't ask this man in the diner how to get there?"

"No."

"That would be what most strangers in a town would do."

Sandra raised her eyes briefly to Depew and said: "It so happens I didn't." Her eyes fell again. "It was easy enough to find Main Street and easy to find the drug store. I parked in front of it. There was a light inside. I went to the door and I was going to knock, but the door was ajar, so I went in." She stopped and drew a deep breath.

"Go on," said Depew. "Did you close the door behind you?"

"Yes. I stood just inside looking around for a few seconds; then I walked down the length of the store. That was when I saw him."

"He was dead?"

"I suppose so."

"What did you do?"

"I think I called out his name, but I knew at the same time that he couldn't hear me."

"What made you so sure he was dead? Did you touch him?"

"No. I just knew."

"I see. Go on. What did you do next?"

She shrugged. "I ran away. I suppose I went into a panic. I hardly remember what I did. All I could think of was the fact that certain people"—her eyes lifted to meet Ed MacIntyre's—"certain people knew that I had tried to kill him in Chicago, and I was afraid I'd be blamed for it now."

"You weren't afraid you'd be blamed for it when you tried it in Chicago?"

"I didn't know what I was doing that time."

"In Chicago?"

"Yes."

"I see. You came to see him in Chicago armed with a gun, but you didn't know what you were doing when you tried to kill him."

"I lost my head."

"You went prepared to lose your head—is that it?"

"I only intended to scare him."

"You contradict yourself," said Depew, rubbing his chin thoughtfully. "However, did you come to Hamsted just to scare him, too?"

"No. I came to see if we couldn't talk sense."

"Why? What did you want to talk about?"

Her hands were folded on her lap, the fingers clasped tightly. "I was still in love with him."

"Uh uh. But you were much more in love with yourself, so you beat it hell-bent-for election when you found him dead. Is that what you want us to understand?"

"I just got seared and ran away. That's all I want you to understand."

"I see. Let's have the rest of it."

"There isn't much more. I drove out of town as fast as I could go and I tried to make a turn too fast and wrecked the car."

"And then you got out of the car and kept on running away, eh?"

"Yes."

"Still in a panic?"

"Yes."

Depew glared down at her and said with savage bitterness:

"In a panic! But not so much in a panic that you didn't think up some pretty smooth lies to tell the chief of police here. You were doing some pretty neat lying for a girl in a panic, weren't you?"

Sandra looked up at Depew with a cold stare. "Lying comes easy to me," she said. "I've done a lot of it in my day."

"Are you lying to me now? Isn't all this story you've told us a cooked up prefabricated lie? Isn't it? Answer me!"

"No. All I've told you here is the truth. Do you think I bribed this restaurant man to give me a phony alibi? Do you think Harry here lied to you?"

"Never mind what I think!" Depew growled. "Answer me one more question: Did you or didn't you tear a paper out of the dead man's hand, a piece of your own note paper, a corner of which was left *in* the dead man's fingers—did you or didn't you?"

"No, I didn't."

"I see. Well, suppose you tell us what was in that letter you wrote to Mr. Tuttle."

The girl's eyes were fixed steadily on Depew. "There wasn't much in it. And yet there was everything in it, I suppose. I asked him if we couldn't make up, if we couldn't let bygones be bygones."

Depew smiled. It was not a pretty smile. "Very sentimental," he said.

The girl looked up quickly, a savage retort ready on her lips. But before she could speak, Hilliard Wells had moved forward quickly, so that he stood between his client and Depew.

"Please! Mr. Depew," he begged. "The important issue—the only issue is where my client was at the time Tuttle was killed. We've shown you where she was—in the diner—so the rest of this is immaterial, isn't it?"

Depew looked at Chief Tomlin and growled something under his breath that nobody heard.

"What's your answer, Mr. Depew?" Wells pressed him.

Depew strode toward the door that led to the anteroom. Paul Hastings, standing with his back to the door, moved to one side. Depew halted, his hand on the door knob. He did not turn about.

"My answer," he said, "will have to wait till I've given more thought to all this, and more investigation. Lock her up again, Tomlin."

IV

Ed MacIntyre walked moodily along, Paul Hastings at his side. A fresh morning breeze from the south whipped away some of the night's fatigue. Ed kicked a stone ahead of him; Hastings carried a cane's-length maple branch and whittled it slowly as he walked.

"How much of an idiot is that idiot?" Ed asked after several moments of silence.

Hastings shrugged. "I don't believe he's an idiot in the technical sense. He's just called that in a fond way by the natives."

Ed nodded. "I'm sure that's plain enough. Maybe he's a little foolish upstairs, but it's a shrewd kind of foolishness. Look: Just before two o'clock Sandra saw no paper in Walt's hand. Our friend the fool was there at quarter of two, by his own evidence. He *says* he didn't see the letter." Hastings shrugged. "Either *he* got the letter, or *she* got it, or the murderer got it, assuming the murderer is neither Sandra nor the fool."

"I think there's more than meets the well-known eye about most of this cock-eyed business," Hastings observed.

Ed nodded slowly. "Do you think the police know or suspect any more than they're saying?" he asked.

Hastings brushed some whittlings off his coat. "Not so far. And I'm in a position to know. I'm pretty implicitly trusted in official quarters. They know I won't spill or print anything they don't want let out. I'll keep you posted, Ed, in confidence of course, and always provided"—there was a grim little humorless smile on his face—"you didn't kill Walt yourself."

"Hey! You don't think they think—"

"I'm not sure," replied Hastings. "A couple of times I didn't like the way Depew was sizing you up. We'll wait and see."

Ed shuddered. They had reached the house. "Come on in," Ed said. "Binnie'll rustle up some bacon and eggs. I'm pooped and I'm hungry and so are you. And for Pete's sake don't tell Binnie they may light on me. She'll go out and kill somebody."

"Okay," said Hastings.

5

THE DREAM

I

After a good breakfast, Ed and Paul Hastings retired to the living room while Binnie cleared away the dishes. Ed gave Hastings a cigarette and Hastings lighted up and yawned.

"I haven't had a full night's sleep in nearly a week now," he complained. "If it hasn't been one thing, it's been another. I'm dead on my feet."

"So am I," said Ed. "Traveling cross country and sleeping in strange beds. And then last night. I'm a wreck."

Hastings' eyes drooped. He pried them open with an effort.

"It's the nervous shock, I suppose," said Ed, "on top of the rest of the fatigue. If you don't mind I'll just stretch out here on the couch."

"Sure," said Hastings. "Go ahead. Do you mind talking a little more? I'd like to interview you for a story of your personal career."

"Why?" demanded Ed, sprawled on his back on dark green divan and already surrounded by a fuzz of sleep. "I'm nobody."

"You're a prominent radio writer," said Hastings. "You're big news in a small town."

"Excuse me," said Ed, "but that's a lot of moosh. Pardon me if I close my eyes for a few seconds."

Ed had a very strange dream. He dreamed that he was walking arm in arm with Walt down a street whose identity he could not determine, in a direction that was neither east nor west, north nor south. At first it seemed that the street was Hollywood

Boulevard and he almost recognized the corner of Hollywood and Vine; but then it became something like Michigan Boulevard with the Wrigley Building looming up like an enormous Polish wedding cake; and Ed and Walt walked through the rotating doors and down the long corridor toward Studio A. Harry Liebowitz was waiting at the door of the studio, washing his thin hands in nervous respect and begging them to do something that wasn't at all clear because it was obliterated by the bellowing of a loudspeaker in the wall. The loudspeaker bore the label: "Mister Lattimer" in bold type. Harry kept bowing obsequiously to the loudspeaker. Ed and Walt marched past Harry, ignoring his voice and his fingers that plucked pleadingly at Ed's sleeve. And just then Walt turned to Ed and said: "You're a prominent radio writer. You're big news in a small town." And Ed said: "That's a lot of moosh. Chicago's no small town." And Walt said: "But this isn't Chicago." And they kept on walking right up to a microphone with the sound-effects man in his corner making the sound of their footsteps as they went. So that Ed thought: "This is cock-eyed. Why does he need to make the sound of our footsteps? Can't we make our own sound with our own footsteps?" And then suddenly, by dint of some Alice in Wonderland trick, they were walking down the main street of the little radio town of Stedham. Ed knew it was Stedham because a sign said so, and furthermore, he recognized the streets he had described in the radio drama. They went strolling in leisurely fashion until they came to a street corner, and there big as life, or probably bigger, was Foss Leonard, the villain of the piece, leaning against the wall of a building on whose door was a sign in blazing letters: Foss Leonard, Attorney. He gave them a savage and superior scowl, for they had made a very unpleasant villain of him, as all good radio villains should be. Then suddenly, as if by some more cock-eyed magic, there appeared beside the villain the little heroine of the drama, Lily Newcomb. She was clutching Foss Leonard's arm and looking up at him in complete adoration mingled with a strange exaggerated unhappiness. Foss Leonard was ignoring her completely. Suddenly Ed yelled out a warning: "Lily! Lily Newcomb! Look out for that man! He's going to

murder you!" But Lily Newcomb did not seem to hear; she merely went on adoring Foss Leonard. who laughed raucously at Ed
and Walt and gave Lily's hand a ten-cent pat. Ed and Walt continued their stroll and soon they approached a man who was old
and gnarled and stooped and wore straggling white whiskers, but
who looked strong as an old oak for all his years. "Hey," said Ed
to Walt, "here comes old Sam Newcomb, Lily's father!" The old
man came plodding on and Ed stopped him by poking a finger
into his chest and shouting at him: "Hey, Mr. Newcomb! You'd
better look out! That man's going to murder your daughter!" Old
man Newcomb merely paused for a moment, looked up at Ed out
of tired blue eyes and said: "Got to get my hay in," and pointed up at a lowering black cloud and went on without another
word. "How do you like that!" said Ed to Walt. "His daughter's
going to be murdered and he's got to get his hay in." They went
a little farther and there was the lovely and plump rich widow
for whom and for whose money the villain would murder little
Lily. The widow was seated by an open window of a flower-
bedecked cottage and she flirted a flower and a ten-grain saccha-
rine smile at Ed and Walt as they went by. "Holy smoke!" said
Ed, "this is a cavalcade—but what a cock-eyed cavalcade! Nobody
pays any attention to the fact that there's going to be a murder
committed right under their noses." And then came the climax
of the whole business. All of a sudden a small-town brass band
in blue and white uniforms came blaring down the street and
right behind them came marching Foss Leonard, carrying a big
sign that screamed: "Listen in tonight at six! Your favorite radio
show! *Home Town!* Come one, come all!" Behind Foss Leonard
marched Lily Newcomb and behind Lily came the rich widow
and behind the widow a whole parade of minor characters out of
the radio show. "Ye gods!" said Ed. "This is positively nuts! We
must be dreaming or something, Walt." But Walt only grinned
and then the parade faded away behind them and suddenly they
were walking in darkness. . . .

Since he couldn't see where he was going, it was just as well
that Binnie roused him.

"Wake up," she said. "Mr. Depew's here to see you."

"Uh?" said Ed abruptly, and came up to a sitting position. There was Depew, tall and lean and hard-jawed. "You want to see me?" inquired Ed. "Where's Paul Hastings? How long have I been asleep?"

"One at a time," said Binnie "You've slept all day long. It's four o'clock in the afternoon. Paul Hastings went away a few minutes after you fell asleep and here's Mr. Depew the assistant district attorney who's going to do something foolish like accusing you of murdering Walt."

"What?" Ed hollered, and after the sound came out his mouth stayed open. He looked up at Depew a little helplessly and saw for the first time that Chief Tomlin was standing in the doorway behind Depew.

"You'd be better off, young lady," said Depew, "if you didn't jump to conclusions."

"Maybe," retorted Binnie belligerently, getting up from the divan to face Depew, "but if you think Ed killed Walt, you're crazy as a bazoo, and while I don't know how crazy a bazoo is, that's just how crazy I think *you* are!"

"Look; said Depew, "I've made no accusations and I certainly haven't told you what I think, for I'm not in the habit of doing that—"

"I can see what you think," said Binnie stiffly, "right in the middle of your face."

"Be that as it may," said Depew, now looking at Ed, "I want to ask you a few questions, Mr. MacIntyre."

"Go ahead," Ed shrugged. "Ask me anything you want. I thought you'd asked me all the questions you wanted to ask."

"Not quite. First, suppose you answer the one your wife thought up. Did you kill Walter Tuttle?"

"I told you so!" declared Binnie, her head held high.

"Pipe down, Toots," Ed cautioned her mildly. "No, I didn't kill Walt Tuttle! Why do you ask that? I thought you understood I had told you everything I know."

"You told us a story, yes; but how much of it is true?"

"Every damned word of it is true!" declared Ed, restraining Binnie by taking hold of her arm. "And I'd like to know why you question it, Mister Depew."

"Look," said Depew quietly, "it won't do you any good to get sore, Mr. MacIntyre. Perhaps I have certain routine questions to ask and perhaps I intend to ask them. Perhaps one of my routine questions, which I hadn't asked you up to now, is whether you killed Walt Tuttle."

"Routine question!" Binnie shouted. "What do you do, go round stopping people on the street, asking them if *they* killed Walt Tuttle? Why don't you ask *me* if *I* killed him?"

"Very well, I will. Did you?"

"Good grief!" said Binnie. "In heaven's name, why should I— or why should Ed—why should either of us kill the best friend we have in the world?"

"Possibly," said Depew in a nonchalant way, his eyes going from Binnie to Ed, "just possibly because Mr. Tuttle had made a will leaving everything he possessed—which was plenty—to you, Mr. MacIntyre."

"What!" Ed got up quickly from the couch, and he was white about the lips. "Walt left everything to me?"

"That's right," Depew nodded. "Didn't you know?"

"No, of course I didn't know!"

Binnie was white about the mouth now too. "I don't believe it," she said.

"Nevertheless it's true," Depew stated, and all of a sudden Binnie began to cry. She began to cry in both her hands, sobbing in a way that racked her frame terribly. Ed stepped forward and turned her about and took her in his arms, not for one moment taking his eyes off Depew. "Walt!" Binnie sobbed. "Poor dear Walt!"

"Just a moment," said Ed to Depew. "How do you happen to know that he left me everything he possessed? I didn't know about it. The will hasn't been probated, has it?"

"No," said Depew.

"Well, I'm no lawyer," Ed declared, "but I'm pretty sure that no one has a right to know what's in that will until it's probated, and after that the heirs are the first ones entitled to know what's in it."

"A district attorney has lots of peculiar rights," said Depew. "However, I don't intend to argue the point one way or another. The fact is, you do inherit, and that gives you a motive for killing Walt Tuttle."

"Oh, rats!" Binnie flung away from Ed and whirled upon Depew. "I've got a motive for killing you right now, but I'm not doing it and I don't intend to, though I'd certainly like to. Ed was Walt's best friend and if you're thinking, as I suppose you are, that even a best friend will kill for money, you can have a look at our bank account and see if we need Walt's money or anybody's money! You and your motives!"

Depew's face was stony.

"Are you arresting me?" Ed asked quietly.

"No," said Depew. "Not yet at any rate. But I'd be careful to be within reach if we should want you."

"Okay," Ed said.

"Now is that all?" Binnie demanded.

"For the time being," Depew nodded.

"Then for the time being, the way out is the same way you came in. Please be good enough to use it."

Mr. Depew bowed slightly and turned and followed Chief Tomlin out of the house.

Ed took Binnie in his arms and patted her shoulder gently. "You're losing your grip, kid," he said. "That's the first time you ever insulted a guest in your own home."

"That's the first time a guest ever accused my husband of murder," she said. "Furthermore, it isn't my home."

"Oh, yes, it is now," said Ed quietly. "Which reminds me. I've got to see a man about a will."

II

The black and gold sign on the glass door on Main Street said Absalom Reynolds, Attorney at Law. Ed pushed open the door and trudged up a long steep flight of dusty gray wooden steps at the head of which another sign with a small arrow directed him down a corridor to the right. He passed several frosted glass doors before he came to the one at the end of the corridor which again proclaimed the existence of Absalom Reynolds, Attorney at Law.

Ed walked in. The outer office was empty. There was a secretary's desk and a typewriter but no secretary. The door to the inner office was closed, but in a moment there were footsteps behind it and the door was opened by Reynolds himself. Today he was not dressed in brown, as yesterday, but in gray tweeds. The slant eyes were raised in a question.

"Mr. Reynolds—" Ed began.

"Yes," said Reynolds. "You wanted to see me, Mr. MacIntyre?"

"If you don't mind."

"Come in. Sit down." He indicated a chair in front of his desk and went round and sat in his own behind it. He leaned back toward the broad window that looked down on Main Street and folded his long lean hands across his stomach. "Yes, Mr. MacIntyre?"

Ed cleared the cobwebs out of his throat. "Mr. Reynolds, you were Walt Tuttle's attorney. Is that right?"

"That's right."

"You arranged the deal on the store, we know. Were you also his attorney to draw up his will?"

"Yes."

"Where is that will?"

"Locked in my safe, right over there."

"It hasn't been probated yet, has it?"

"No."

Ed paused and leaned forward, elbows on the arms of the chair, and he pointed his next question straight between Reynolds' slant eyes. "Then how does it happen that the district attorney knows the contents of that will?"

The slant eyes went up. The head was cocked a little on one side. "Does he know the contents?"

"You know damn well he does," Ed replied quietly. "He told me about the contents. I inherit everything Walt had—and that's a motive for murder. Get it?"

"Rubbish!" said Reynolds, smiling pleasantly. "That's a lot of rubbish."

"It may be rubbish to you but to me it's just hemp rope."

Reynolds still smiled. "It's the electric chair in this state, Mr. MacIntyre," he said.

There was a cold fury in Ed. "The method be damned!" he said. "What right did you have to tell the district attorney what was in that will? You were Walt's confidential agent, his attorney, and you owed him a duty, a professional duty. You had no right to tell Depew what was in that will!"

"Just a moment, please." Reynolds took hold of the arms of his chair and pulled himself toward Ed. "Let's take this up a step at a time. In the first place, I have not said that I told the district attorney or anybody else what was in the will—"

"Well, it stands to reason—"

"In the second place, though I admit nothing, let us consider what my professional duty might be. My client is murdered. There is a motive for murder in my client's will. The man who murdered him may escape if the police do not know of this motive at once. What would *you* say my professional duty would be under those circumstances?"

Ed slowly got to his feet. "So you think I murdered him," he said. "Well, you can go straight to hell, which is probably where you'll go anyway, by the ugly look of you. But I'll bet you forty dollars I can have you disbarred for your cheap violation of duty and, by God, I've got a good mind to see that it's done!"

Reynolds shrugged and showed empty hands. "Anything you say, Mr. MacIntyre. I'm still admitting nothing. And if you'll come around some other day when you aren't so hot under the collar maybe I'll take that little forty-dollar bet." He rose. "Good day, Mr. MacIntyre. I'm busy. I have work to do."

III

Ed walked wearily into the house, threw his hat across the living room and sat down in a big armchair. Binnie curled up in his lap.

"What happened?"

He told her about Reynolds.

"Are you going to try to have him disbarred?"

Ed drew a deep breath. "No. I suppose I couldn't do it. And besides, I suppose he thought he was doing the right thing by Walt. I guess we'd have done the same thing in his place."

"Just the same," said Binnie, "I intend to cut him dead when I see him. And if that district attorney comes around here again, accusing you—"

"I think you'd better go easy on him," Ed warned. "In a way he's a good guy."

"If that's your idea of a good guy—"

"Well, he's a good guy for not arresting me. I've been thinking about it. No, he hasn't got anything on me, but look, sister, he's got everything to work with if he wants to go to work: the will; where was I when Walt was killed—"

"I'm a witness as to that!"

"A heck of a lot they'd believe what *you* said about it."

"Well, why *don't* they arrest you, then, if you think they've got so much to work on?"

"I don't know," Ed shrugged. "Maybe they want to do the old trick of leaving me enough rope to hang myself."

Binnie got up in a white rage and strode up and down the room like a wooden doll. "Of all the hang-dang crazy fool situations, this is the prize! We come to a nice little town for a nice little rest for the rest of our nice little lives, and Walt gets murdered and someone accuses my husband of doing it! Grapenuts! I want to go back to Hollywood where it isn't so nice and there isn't any rest and the worst thing you can do is go respectfully mad. But *here—!*"

Ed tripped her up as she marched past and jerked her into his lap. "Look, cookie," he said, "I was accused as a feeler. I'm not arrested—yet. Now I'm sure of one thing. The most important thing we have to do is to keep our heads. How about it?"

She let out a sharp breath of disgust. "Oh, very well! But what do we do in the meantime, twiddle our thumbs-dee-dee?"

"No," Ed replied. "We follow the best lead to Walt's murderer."

"And what is the best lead?"

"I'm not sure," Ed said, "but for a starter I'd like to have another little talk with our good friend Dodo Brown."

6
THE NOTE FROM JACOB BURDICK

I

After dinner Ed drove downtown to find Dodo Brown, but there was no Dodo to be seen. Ed dropped in at the store. The fountain was jammed and the rest of the store was crowded. He watched the slick, sleek Carl Benjamin moving like an efficient machine, handling customers and sales with a natural knack perfected by long practice. He smiled often, talked softly and smoothly, exuded an air of complete competence, wrapped packages with a swift deftness, greeted customers and bade good evening to those who departed without spoiling the rhythm of the task immediately at hand. He gave Ed a quick impersonal greeting, then ignored him completely.

Ed wandered into the prescription department at the rear. The efficient Carl had already hired another pharmacist to take Oscar Batchelder's place. He was an old man with a tired grin, Ora Moosehead by name. He seemed to know who Ed was and introduced himself. Ed watched him make up a prescription, then went out into the front of the store again.

Jenny the redhead was mixing sodas and making sundaes with a sure, quick hand and giving off sparks of wit to the men at the fountain, who seemed to enjoy her humor and her drinks. The soda draft arm hissed and the cash registers played their tune, and though there may have been some talk about Walt's death—there probably was, for customers turned to look at the place where Walt had died—oddly enough there was no undercurrent of tragedy.

He was able to intercept Carl Benjamin long enough to learn that Dodo Brown had not been in the store that day. After a little while Ed wandered out of the store and up and down Main Street a few times, but there was no Dodo, so Ed drove home.

A big black limousine was parked in front of the house. Ed ran his car into the garage and went into the house to find Binnie entertaining Slade Lattimer, Sandra Lattimer, Harry Liebowitz, an attorney named Clyde Crouse who was, Ed knew, one of the most capable criminal lawyers in Chicago, a Dr. Cathcart from Boston, and Paul Hastings.

"Hello, Sandra," Ed said. "Glad to see you're out. How permanent is it?"

It seems it was permanent on one condition. There was Clyde Crouse's pledge to return her to the town if she should be wanted later. Concerning her release, Dr. Cathcart, a former medical examiner and medico-legal authority, had convinced the district attorney that the temperature of Walt's body, as recorded by the local medical examiner at the time of examination at two-thirty in the morning, was such that Walt must have been dead at least since midnight; that quite certainly he was murdered during the time that Sandra was in the diner with Harry Liebowitz and with the counterman as witness to the fact that she was there. And since this was in complete agreement with the medical examiner's decision, Depew knew better than to take a case like that into the criminal courts.

Ed sighed, listening and looking at the floor. Would Depew know better than to take *him* into the criminal courts?

Lattimer was speaking now. "MacIntyre," he said, and Ed looked up through a wall of fatigue. "MacIntyre, we're going back to Chicago tonight. I want you to know there are no hard feelings on my side for anything that's happened between us. I'm sorry about Tuttle, terribly sorry. I want you to know that if you can see your way to coming back to us, we'd like to have you."

Ed shook his head slowly. "No, thanks. I don't think I want any more radio without Walt."

Harry Liebowitz was on his feet. "Ed, if you won't come back, will you at least advise us on the script? The hams we've got doing it now are wrecking it. Can we talk the layout over before we go back?"

"Sure," said Ed. "Sure."

"Now?"

"Okay," Ed replied, and got up. "Come on into the den. If you'll excuse us," he said to the rest of them.

"I'll meet you at the inn as soon as I can," Harry said to Lattimer. Lattimer nodded and got to his feet. Ed and Harry started for the den.

Paul Hastings said apologetically: "If it's only about the radio script and nothing personal, your public's interested in a conference like that."

"Sure, Paul," Ed said. "Come along."

II

The big German shepherd heard scampering footsteps on the front walk, leaped out of a corner and shot like an arrow for the front windows. The outraged ferocity of his bark had Ed out of his chair at a bound.

"Quiet, Mike! Shut up, Mike!" He drew aside the curtains and looked out. A small figure—it might have been a boy, or a girl in slacks—was darting down the steps of the porch. A car, cruising slowly down the street, suddenly speeded up, shot past the house and vanished, its light abruptly extinguished. The boy—or girl—vanished in the dark in the direction opposite to that in which the car had gone.

Mike was racing from window to window in a frenzy, his bark ear-splitting. Binnie jumped up and went for him. "For Pete's sake, Mike, shut your big mouth!" She clamped her hands on his jaw, hung onto him and smothered his bark. "What's the matter, Ed? Anybody out there?"

Ed was still looking out. "Somebody ran up onto the porch and then ran down again. A boy or a girl. And a car turned off its lights and went hell-bent past. Hold onto him."

He went to the door, opened it and looked out. In the rectangle of light that fell out obliquely onto the floor of the porch he saw a folded piece of paper.

"Turned off its lights?" Binnie was saying. "Why?"

"How do I know why? Maybe so I couldn't get his number."
He picked up the piece of paper and brought it into the house,
closed the door behind him and held up the paper for Binnie to
see.

"Now what in the name of time is that?" Binnie asked.

Ed opened it. It was a single sheet of soiled writing paper,
cheap grade, with a narrow pale blue border. On it was written
in pencil by a hand that had labored prodigiously to produce a
crude scrawl of words: "Dear Sir:—I am sending you this message. I have got to see you quick. I want you should meet me,
please, at Waterbury Corner alongside the old wite house on the
north side of house. It is about Walt Tuttle dying. I am sorry to
have to ask you to come and see me but this is because I do not
dare to come there because I think I am being watched. Please
come as soon as you get this. (Signed) Jacob Burdick."

Binnie was at his side, reading. "No, Ed," she said firmly.

"No what?" Ed asked, still staring at the letter, a frown between his eyes.

"You're *not* going to the old white house on the north side of
house. This is something peculiar and I don't trust it." Ed was
silent. "You hear me?"

"I hear you." He continued thoughtfully to consider the note.
Then he went to the console table in the hall and picked up his
hat. Binnie fled to the door and stood with her back against it,
feet planted wide, her fists on her hips.

"Ed, you're not going!"

Ed put the note into his pocket and stood looking down at
her. "Look, honey," he said, "cut out the melodramatic salami,
will you? There are certain things you have to do and you do
them!"

"You're *not* going out in this dark to a place you don't know
anything about and meet a man you don't know! It might be a
trap!"

"Don't talk like a radio script, will you?" he said patiently.

"I'm not talking like a radio script. If you go, Ed, I'll—I'll—"

"You'll what?" he grinned.

"I'll—I'll—" She floundered desperately. "Well. I won't be here when you get back—*if* you get back! I'll take the first train not for Chicago but back to Hollywood. You know very well that Zeke Steuben says I can be his secretary any time I want the job."

"Zeke Steuben be damned," said Ed good-naturedly but in dead earnest. "Look, Binnie, I can't overlook this thing. Will you be satisfied if I get the chief of police to go along with me?"

Binnie pouted, thinking it over. "Well," she said hesitantly, "all right. But no funny business. You get the chief to go along or you don't go."

"Okay." He planted a kiss where she still pouted.

"Maybe I'd better go along!" she decided suddenly.

"Sure," he declared. "You go along and keep that armchair warm. Right over there. Go on now. Beat it."

"But, Ed—"

"Nix. I'll be back as soon as I can."

He opened the door and went out.

"Well, you be careful!" she warned.

"I will," he promised.

III

Chief Tomlin read the note and got to his feet. "How long ago'd you get it?"

"Fifteen minutes ago—less."

"Okay, come on." They went but to the sidewalk. "We'll take your car."

Driving, Ed queried, "Who's this Burdick anyhow?"

"Just an old man," said the chief. "Nobody special."

Ed drove half a mile out of town on a dark country road before the chief motioned ahead to a crossroad.

"That's Waterbury Corner. Swing right. There's the white house."

Ed made the turn and brought the car to a stop. The white house sat back alone from the road on broad haunches like a sprawling animal in the night gloom. "Anybody live here?" Ed asked.

"Nope," said the chief, getting out. "Come on."

They walked through a thicket of tall grass and low brush, heading for the right side of the house.

"This is north," said the chief. They stared into the darkness for some sign of the man who was to wait here.

"I don't see anybody," Ed said.

"Nope." They walked along the north side of the house. "Nope. Nobody." They walked to the northeast corner. The moon lay behind smoky clouds.

"Call him," said the chief.

"Burdick," Ed called. "Jacob Burdick!" There was no answer. They went on walking, circled the house, returned to the north side.

"That's funny," Ed said.

The chief took a flashlight out of his pocket and played its light on the ground as they went on slowly.

"Look!" The chief stopped, pointing, then stooped to pick up the dead butt of a crude handmade cigarette.

"There's another," said Ed. "And one more." There were five altogether.

"That's Burdick all right," said Chief Tomlin. "He rolls his own. He was smoking and waiting." His flashlight moved up from the ground.

"But where is he now?"

"Look!" said the chief again. His light, moving along the wall of the house, jerked to a stop. "Look at that!" He moved quickly to the wall and his long finger stabbed at what his light had found. "That's a bullet!" he said. "And it's a brand-new bullet hole. See where the broken wood around it's fresh and clean?"

"Meaning what?" Ed asked.

"Well, no one plugged him, because there's no blood. But somebody came down close and scared him off."

"Where does he live? Let's go there. Maybe we'll find him."

"Okay," said the chief. "Come on." They drove back toward town, then, half a mile from the center, turned west on a poor dirt road. The car bounced in ruts on a road lined with pines until they came to a small clearing. A very old and fat mongrel with collie strain predominating came waddling out into the headlights, barking ferociously. Ed brought the car to a stop and the chief got out at once to meet the dog. The mongrel came to a slow halt as the chief held out his hand and said quietly: "Pipe down, Fatso. Come here."

The dog stopped barking and came forward now with his tail wagging. He put his head under the chief's hand to get it scratched. Performing the requested office, the chief called out: "Jake! Jake Burdick, you home?"

But the house, a sorry one-story shack, was dark and there was no reply from the darkness.

The chief went forward, the dog trotting at his heels and nuzzling his palm. Tomlin stopped at the front door and banged on it with a bony fist. "Jake! Hey, Jake, you home? Jake, this is Al Tomlin. If you're in there, Jake, speak up. I'm out here with Mister MacIntyre."

There was no answer. The chief walked, back to the car. There was a frown on his face. "Something's funny," he said "I don't like the looks of it. I don't get it, but I don't like the looks of it." He gave the dog a final pat and got into the car, where he sat silent and thoughtful for a few seconds. Then he shrugged. "I don't get it," he said. "Let's go back to town."

They were driving back to the center of town and Ed was thinking about Jacob Burdick. "What's the lowdown on this Burdick?" he asked after a brief spell of silence.

The chief took a briar pipe out of one pocket and a worn leather pouch out of the other. He filled his pipe slowly, put it in his mouth and slid the pouch back into his pocket. Then he searched carefully in several pockets for a match before he found one and lighted up so that red coals glowed in the briar bowl. He sent forth enormous clouds of smoke and still Ed's question went unanswered. Then at last Tomlin said: "I don't know what to say, MacIntyre. Offhand I'd say there ain't any real lowdown on Burdick. He's just a plain everyday simple man. Let's see how far back he goes. He came to this town here all of thirty years ago. I remember him when he came. He was from down Maine, I guess. About forty years old then. Came and opened up a little grocery store. Used to be some rumors about him being a wealthy man who'd gone broke and saved just enough to open the little store. I remember that store, plain as if it was yesterday. The kids used to like to hang out there and us young fellers used to buy our tobacco there. Jake went along all right for about fifteen years, then his credit business got bigger than his cash business and the people that owed him didn't pay, so he folded up and went to work for somebody else. He worked in maybe half a dozen of the stores in town for different lengths of time over about another fifteen years, sort of going downhill and looking seedier all the time, lettin' his mustache grow kind of straggy—"

"Did he know Walt Tuttle?" Ed broke in.

"I don't know, but he probably did. I suppose Jake knew all the kids, or anyway all the kids knew old Jake."

"Can you think of any connection between them, anything that might point up a reason for Burdick's knowing anything about Walt's death?"

The chief pondered that for several seconds, then shook his head slowly. "Can't think of anything," he said.

"Look," said Ed. "Walt was murdered in the store, behind closed doors. Burdick knows something about the murder. Either he saw the murderer go into the store or leave the store, or he knows some fact that caused the murderer to go to the store and kill Walt. There's some connection between Burdick and the killer or between Burdick and Walt, some connection that made it possible for Burdick to know something about Walt's death. You're the chief of police. You're supposed to know the connections between people in a small town, aren't you?"

"Yes and no. A man can't know everything, even in a small town."

"Can't you put your finger on anything, no matter how insignificant or remote?"

The chief was thinking again. "No," he answered finally. "I don't know a thing."

7
EXIT JACOB BURDICK

I

Walt Tuttle's funeral was the next day. It was a dull, lowering, raw day with a sharp east wind that bore the threat of rain.

Paul Hastings and Ed were pallbearers; the others were men who remembered Walt from his boyhood days in the town. The services in the funeral parlor were brief enough but too long for Ed, to whom every moment was slow torture. To Ed's surprise Sandra Lattimer and Harry Liebowitz were there. He had thought they had gone back to Chicago. There was no sign of Slade Lattimer.

The ride to the cemetery, on the outskirts of the town, was deadly slow. Binnie, sitting beside Ed, gripped his hand all the way. She was white-faced, strained with fatigue, and her eyes did not meet Ed's until the car in which they rode, following the hearse up a little rise into the cemetery, came to a stop and Ed got out to do his last service for Walt.

They took the casket out of the hearse and carried it to the open grave, and the mourners, many of them people who had come merely out of curiosity to the grave of a murdered man, followed after the coffin in little silent groups.

Binnie was at Ed's side again. The minister, at the head of the grave, cleared his throat and turned the fluttering pages of his prayer book. Ed's eyes wandered away from the coffin and looked slowly at the faces of the people there. He was a little shocked—and yet not wholly surprised—to see Assistant District Attorney Depew and Chief Tomlin. Depew stood with topcoat collar turned up, hands thrust deep in his trousers pockets, his head down a little, but his eyes seeing all that went on about him. Tomlin, in plain clothes, stared up at the gray sky.

The wind was down and the cold mist had grown heavier. It went through clothes into the bones.

The minister cleared his throat again. "Man that is born of woman hath but a short time to live, and is full of misery. He cometh up, and is cut down, like a flower; he fleeth as it were a shadow, and never continueth in one way. . . ."

From the rise on which they stood Ed could see the road that led up from the town. It ran like a gray frayed-edged ribbon and disappeared behind some pine trees. Walt's last road. Moisture filled Ed's eyes, and it was through this blur that he saw the figure of a man come around the curve at an awkward limping trot.

He thought nothing of the man's identity at first, until Paul Hastings, at Ed's side, muttered: "Dodo Brown."

It was indeed Dodo. He came trotting on. He stumbled once and almost fell, regained his balance and picked up his gait. He came into the cemetery and Ed could see that he was panting hard.

"Thou knowest, Lord, the secrets of our hearts; shut not thy merciful ears to our prayer; but spare us, Lord most holy, O God most mighty; suffer us not, at our last hour, for any pains of death, to fall from thee. . . ."

Dodo's trot had become a walk. He neared the crowd surrounding the grave, his eyes searching the faces anxiously. At length he espied Ed and his face lighted. He walked, loose and shambling, behind mourners who stirred uneasily at his intrusion and several of them turned to see who it was. Dodo edged his way through the knot of people who stood behind Ed, Binnie and Paul Hastings and came to a halt behind Ed. Ed did not turn. He could hear the hard breathing of the boy, and suddenly felt a touch on his hand as something was pressed into his fingers. He turned then, as did Binnie and Paul Hastings, to look at Dodo. There was a strange, shrewd look in the boy's eyes, a look of cunning that half belied, half accented the dullness of his mind. Ed glanced down. There was a dirty, many-times-folded square of paper in his hand. Dodo looked at the paper and then at Ed; then he backed away into the crowd.

The undertaker cast a shovelful of earth upon the coffin.

"Unto Almighty God we commend the soul of our brother departed, and we commit his body to the ground; earth to earth, ashes to ashes, dust to dust. . . ."

Ed slowly unfolded the paper. It was a sheet of cheap ruled writing paper and on it was a second message from Jacob Burdick. As Ed's eyes read the message he turned almost involuntarily toward Paul Hastings, but then stopped as his eyes caught up with the last words of the message: "Don't tell *nobody* and come alone. Don't tell *nobody!*"

Ed folded the note and put it in his pocket. Binnie looked up at him quizzically. He ignored her glance, his eyes on the minister.

"Our Father, who art in heaven, hallowed be thy Name. Thy kingdom come, Thy will be done, on earth as it is in heaven. Give us this day our daily bread. And forgive us our trespasses, as we forgive those who trespass against us. And lead us not into temptation, but deliver us from evil. Amen."

There was an uneasy stirring among the mourners. Those on the outer fringe of the group turned slowly and walked away toward their cars. The rest followed.

Except for the undertaker's men, only Ed and Binnie, Paul Hastings, Depew, and Tomlin remained. Harry Liebowitz and Sandra had gone. Depew and Tomlin remained in conference, hands thrust into their pockets, heads down.

Hastings touched Ed's arm. "Shall we go?"

They went down to the car. It was only when they drove out of the gates onto the road that Binnie began to cry. She wept silently, in both hands. Neither Ed nor Paul Hastings said a word.

II

"Dear Sir:—I am sending you another message as we did not meet before as planned. I was there alright like I said I would, but an atempt was made on my life and so I had to get away and could not meet you. I am sorry. Please meet me at a different place tonight. If you will come down Fuller's Road to the end and stand under the big oak tree at ten oclock, I will be watching from somewheres nearby. When I am sure that all is well I will join you. Please do not be mad at me for taking precautions as it is absolutely necesary. Please do no fale me ten o'clock. (Signed) J. B."

Ed drove slowly down Main Street through a torrent of wind-driven rain. A casual question at the newsstand near the diner had produced information concerning Fuller's Road. It ran south off Main Street a quarter of a mile from the center of town. On Main Street, Ed's was the only car heading east. A few cars came toward him, their headlights blurred yellow gold by silver rain. Bucketsful splashed up at Ed's windshield and his closed windows as car passed car. Then Ed's car was alone and he slowed to read a street sign, made out "Fuller's Road" in his headlights and swung right down the road. It was a rutty, bumpy, deluged road. The car jerked in and out of deep tracks and the going looked worse ahead.

Ed drove off the road onto a little rising bank on the right, turned off motor and lights and got out, first shoving into his pocket the big flashlight that was clamped to the steering post. Then, with coat buttoned up to his chin and chin deep in the up-turned collar, he sloshed off through the water and mud, flash-light guiding the way.

The muck was as sticky as chewing gum. The road went up-hill a little and the rain poured down the slope as down a drain trough. Ed fought wind and torrent to the top of a rise where suddenly the road became harder, with no ruts and scarcely any mud; the rain beat upon it and made of it a sluiceway, and Ed walked on faster.

His head was still down against the onslaught and his light pointed only a foot or two ahead of him, so he had no warning save that which his ears gave him. And his ears, in the roar of the tempest, gave him only the faintest margin of warning, but it was enough.

He threw up his head, gasping in the blast of wind and rain that snatched his breath. A motor roared in a slightly different

pitch from the voice of the storm—a motor that bore down upon
him like a plunging bull. Momentarily it was only a black shape
against the blacker night. Then, as he came to a frozen halt,
headlights, suddenly switched on, leaped out of the dark, full and
piercing and blinding. But if these stabbing lights were intended
to hold him for the kill, they succeeded only in frustrating their
purpose. Ed leaped like a startled rabbit, plunged headlong off
the road, rolled through mud and water down a sandy slope and
finished face down in a puddle of cool water.

He heard the angry song of the car that fled past. It was in
second gear and the motor screamed to the driving pressure of a
wide-open throttle. Ed made no attempt to scramble back to the
road in the hope of reading the license plate. He merely pushed
himself into a sitting position and wiped the muddy water from
his face with both hands and began to swear savagely. The sound
of the car blended quickly again with the sound of the storm. Ed
got to his feet, climbed up the bank onto the road and began to
grope about for his flashlight, found it, pressed the button and
was soothed a little to find that it shot forth its white light.

Several hundred yards farther on, Fuller's road came to dead
end marked by a log fence with a field beyond. An enormous oak
stood at the roadside. Ed stood under it, sheltered a little from
the rain, and played his light on the ground, the bushes, the trees
about him.

"Burdick!" The wind threw the name back in his face. "Hey,
Burdick! Jacob Burdick!" He began to walk back and forth,
throwing the light on the ground, looking for footprints in the
mud. There were none but his own. He looked at his watch. He
was five minutes late. It was five minutes past ten. "Burdick!"

No answer.

He walked around the tree and a little distance each way
along the edge of the field. He looked over the fence as he went
along, then returned to the shelter of the oak, lighted a cigarette
and waited in silence, his flashlight dark. At ten-thirty he called
Burdick's name once more, then started back down the road to
his car. The rain was beginning to let up a little. Walking with it
at his back was less disagreeable. When he left the solid road and

came to the muddy section, he found the tracks of the car that had tried to run him down, but they were blurred and vanishing.

Reaching his own car, he kicked the mud off his feet on the running board, got in, swung the car around and headed back to Main Street. There he turned east and headed for the place where Burdick lived. The rain was over now and each night sound stood alone, undimmed by the storm. A dog was howling a high, wolf call. Ed drove his car onto the clearing in front of Burdick's shack, pulled up ten yards from the door, and sat quite still. The shack was dark. The dog, Fatso, sat on the doorstep with his head thrown back, sending his long morbid note up to the black sky. The sound gave Ed a shiver that had nothing to do with his wet clothes. He got out of the car and approached the dog.

"Come here, Fatso."

The dog paid no attention to him, paused only for breath, then began to howl again.

Ed called, "Burdick," twice. The dog stopped howling and began to whimper. Ed squatted down beside him and stroked his head. The dog nuzzled into Ed's hand momentarily, then got up and went walking off slowly, whining as he went.

"Burdick!" Ed rattled the door. It was locked. The dog stopped briefly, looked back at the sound, then walked away into the darkness.

Ed walked around the shack, shot his light through a window. Table . . . chair . . . bed . . . cupboard . . . a stack of newspapers, a stack of magazines, a couple of books on a lone shelf—but no Burdick.

Suddenly the dog began to howl again, a little distance away. Ed went around to the clearing. "Fatso!" The dog came back at a trot this time. He came out of the dark into the glare of the headlights and stopped at Ed's feet, whimpering softly. After a moment or two Ed turned away and walked toward the place where Fatso had come out of the darkness. His flashlight showed him a narrow path through low bushes, a path down a dark slope. He heard a soft panting behind him; the dog was there, plodding along.

At the foot of the slope the path turned to the right. Ed stopped and lifted his light ahead of him. Twenty yards away was a small shed, slant-roofed, leaning awkwardly to one side. The dog trotted on ahead now; he went to the door of the shed and began to scratch at it. Then he sat down and began to howl. Ed went for the shed at a run. "Burdick!"

He threw open the door of the shed. It was damp and musty inside. Ed threw his light over dirt-strewn wood planks that made the floor, and up and down the walls. Whatever the shed had been used for once, it had gone into disuse now. The place was bare.

Suddenly the dog flung himself over the threshold and began to scratch frantically at the flooring.

"Look out, Fatso." Ed pushed the dog away, reached down and got his fingers into the crack between two planks; he pulled and a heavy plank came up and fell over with a bang. He yanked at another; that came away too. He stepped over the opening and pulled one up on the other side. Then he got down on his hands and knees, flashlight looking down into the loose dirt beneath the flooring. With one hand he began to paw away the dirt. In a moment he struck something that did not yield. He grasped at it. There was heavy cloth, as of a coat, and a button between his fingers. The dog was crying pitifully as Ed crawled on his knees for a few feet and began to sweep dirt away again.

His fingers slowed, and his stomach writhed. He had uncovered a face.

8

THE CAR WITHOUT LIGHTS

I

Ed stopped first at the diner and phoned Hastings at his home. "Hell's about to pop all around me," he said breathlessly. "I can use moral support if you have any to offer."

"What's happened now?" Hastings asked.

Ed took a deep breath and said quietly: "Burdick's dead. I just found him."

There was a moment of silence at the other end. Then: "You mean you haven't reported it?" Hastings asked.

"Not yet. I'm going down now."

"Where are you going—chief's office?"

"If he's there."

"He's probably there. I'll meet you there in ten minutes."

II

An hour later the chief walked into his office, sat down, leaned back in his chair, put his feet on his desk and began to whittle a match stick. "All right, MacIntyre, you can go home," he said.

Ed stared at the chief and then at Hastings and back at the chief again. "Now don't look at me as if you thought I was nuts," the chief said. "I said you could go home."

"Wait a minute," Ed said. "You aren't arresting me nor even asking me to stay till the D. A. gets here? Aren't you slipping, Chief? I found the first body and just found this one—remember? You're sure I'm not pinched?"

The chief smiled grimly. "Look, brother, I'm not the biggest dope in the world. I happen to know you couldn't have killed Burdick."

"Do you? How do you?"

"Well," Tomlin replied, pausing to extricate a stub born sliver of food from the back of his mouth, "in the first place, the doctor says Burdick has been dead several hours. He got shot maybe five-six hours ago. That puts us back to six or seven o'clock."

"So what?" Ed demanded. "What's so beautiful about six or seven o'clock? Maybe that's when I get my blood-thirstiest."

"Stop asking for trouble," the chief went on. "I'm trying to tell you. Brother, I've had a man on your tail practically every minute since the death of Walter Tuttle and—"

"You've had a *what?*"

"You heard me. And it's a good thing for you I did. Otherwise maybe I *would* slap you in for killing Burdick. I handed you an alibi, that's what *I* did."

Ed sat back, relieved. He looked at Hastings, who sat quietly in a corner, legs crossed, his pipe giving off lazy blue smoke.

"Wait a minute," Hastings said. "You had a tail on him. Presumably the tail followed him up to his rendezvous tonight. Why didn't he do something when the murderer's car tried to run MacIntyre down?"

The chief smiled ruefully. "He wasn't there then," he said. "He had a baby at nine o'clock and I let him go to the hospital to see his wife." He looked at Ed. "You've been on your own since nine."

Ed smiled for the first time that night. "Kind of risky, wasn't it?" he said. "I might have murdered half of your town."

"Sure," said the chief. "You might, but you didn't."

"But you still think I might have killed Walt Tuttle?"

"Well, I don't know now," the chief replied slowly.

"Putting a tail on me says you think I did."

"Not necessarily. Sometimes we do things just sort of routine-like."

"I see. And what—sort of routine-like—did you find out about the tracks of the car that tried to kill me?"

"Nothing," replied the chief. "The rain saw to that. The rain wiped out every trace of everything."

"Can you suggest any way to find out whose car it was?"

Tomlin shrugged. "No trace."

"That's fine," Ed said gloomily. "Every time I go out now I can expect a car to bump me off."

There was a knock at the door and Officer Johnny Brewer put his head in. "There's a kid here, Chief, says he's the one that took the first note from Jake Burdick to MacIntyre."

"Good!" said the chief, sitting up. "Send him in." The door opened wider to admit a thin, straw-haired boy of fourteen. His pale blue eyes were wide and his mouth was open as he looked from the chief to Ed and Hastings and then back to the chief. "Come in, son. Stand over there."

"Yes, sir."

"You're Tom Halleck's boy, ain't you?"

"Yes, sir."

"Don't be afraid. Last night you took a note from Mr. Burdick to the house where this gentleman lives?" He waved a long finger at Ed.

"Yes, sir. My dad heard they were sayin' around town they wanted to know who brought the note from Mr. Burdick, so when I told my dad he told me I'd have to come down here and see you."

"Pretty late for you to be out, ain't it?"

"Yes, sir. My dad drove me down. He's waitin' outside."

"What's your name?"

"Dan."

"All right, Dan. Tell us what happened with Mr. Burdick."

"Yes, sir. I didn't do anything wrong. I was just down on Main Street and I went into Carrie's Ice Cream Place and when I came out I was walking up Main Street, going home, and Mr. Burdick stepped out of the alley there and asked me would I take a note up to the big white house on Walden Street for a nickel, and I said I would."

"Okay. Did he say anything else?"

"No, sir. He gave me a nickel and a piece of paper all folded up and he told me all I had to do was give the note to Mr. Mac-Intyre and not to tell anybody else where I was going and then he ducked down the alley quick."

"Why did he duck down the alley quick?"

"I don't know. He kind of acted like he was sorta scared, but I didn't see anything to be scared about—not right then."

"When did you see something to be scared about?"

"When I got down to Ash Street."

"What did you see there?"

The boy gulped. "There was a car. It was coming along on the other side of the street, and it didn't have any lights on."

"Why did that scare you?"

"I don't know—only it was so dark in the street and the car kept comin' slow, awful slow, just stayin' back of me."

"Go ahead."

"Well, when I turned down Walden Street, the car turned down too; and then all of a sudden I thought maybe this was what Mr. Burdick was scared of, so I began to run as fast as I could go. I ran up on the porch of the big white house and threw the note in front of the door and ran down the steps again and ran back the way I came, as fast as I could."

"What did the car do?"

"It speeded up and drove off."

"Not following you any more?"

"No, sir. It put on its lights and kept on going the way it was going and I was running back the way I came."

"And you don't have any idea whose car it was or who was driving it?"

"No, sir."

"Did you see Mr. Burdick after that—at all?"

"No, sir. I never seen him since."

"Okay, son. Now just one more question. Did you read the note Mr. Burdick gave you?"

"No, sir."

"All right, son. That's all. Thanks for coming down. Thank your dad for bringing you."

"Yes, sir."

The boy went out. There was a brief silence. "Which leaves you," Hastings pointed out, "right where you were before."

"Not exactly," Ed pointed out. "In the first place, it corroborates my story about the first note. In the second place, it gives a pretty good picture of what happened afterwards."

"What, for instance?" the chief inquired.

"Figure it out," Ed said. "Whoever was in the car doubled back and picked up Burdick's trail somewhere, followed him and prevented our first rendezvous by taking a shot at him."

"Which don't add a damn thing to what we know," the chief said with a yawn. "You look tired, MacIntyre. Why don't you go home and finish drying out your clothes and go to bed."

"Suits me fine," Ed said, and he sneezed. "Probably all I've got out of this is a little pneumonia, which, of course, with all these murders going on, doesn't amount to anything at all."

III

But Ed didn't go home. He went looking for the place where Dodo Brown lived. The night man at the diner told him that Dodo lived in a room in a tenement house on the north side. Ed found it several minutes later. It was a dark, two-story, flat-roofed structure with a big front porch. There were two entrances. In a corner of the porch, seated in the darkness, an old man rocked in a creaking rocker and smoked a glowing pipe. "Upstairs. That door," he said to Ed. "Last room on the right."

Ed went up dark stairs that creaked under his feet and along a corridor as dark as the stairs. There was a symphony of muffled snoring from behind the various doors. Ed threw the beam from, his flashlight on the door on the right at the end of the corridor. From within came a snore that was formidable. Ed knocked, but the snore neither stopped nor abated a decibel. Ed knocked again, then tried the knob. The door was unlocked.

Ed went in, closed the door behind him. "Dodo."

There was a bed, a table, a dresser, a chair, no rug. On the bed, sprawled on his back, was Dodo Brown, minus only shoes and suit coat, without a bedcover. Ed reached for an electric light bulb that dangled from the ceiling. It was a poor, pale light that responded. Dodo frowned at the light in his sleep and turned on his side away from it. His snoring stopped.

"Dodo." Ed walked over to the bed. "Dodo, wake up." The boy muttered. "Dodo, wake up. I want to talk to you." The boy rolled over slowly and his eyes opened a little and he looked up at Ed with no sign of recognition. He muttered again and closed his eyes once more. "Dodo, it's Mr. MacIntyre. I want to talk to you. I'll buy you another strawberry ice cream soda."

The beady little eyes opened again and remained open. "Uh?"

Ed sat down beside him. "Dodo, I want to ask you a few questions."

The boy eyed him sullenly. "You ain't bought me my strawrberry ice cream sodas yet. You promised me three of 'em. I ain't got 'em yet."

Ed reached into his pocket for a pencil and an old envelope. He scribbled a few words on it and put it in Dodo's hand. "Here. You give them this. It's good for all the sodas I owe you."

The eyes lighted dimly. The boy shoved the paper inside his shirt.

"Dodo, you brought me a note this morning at the graveyard. Where did you get it?"

The eyes flickered. He was almost asleep again.

"Where'd you get the note, Dodo?" Ed shook him.

"The note? . . . Got it from Jake. Old Jake Burdick."

"Dodo, don't go to sleep again. Where was Jake when he gave it to you? Where were you? Where were you both?"

"Uh?"

"Where did he give you the note? Was it up at Jake's place? Was it down here? Where was it? Where were you?"

"Up the pool room."

"What pool room? Where?"

"We only got one pool room. Haggerty's."

"Where is Haggerty's?"

"Main Street."

"Look, Dodo, don't go to sleep. Who was around, who was near when you got the note at the pool room?"

"Uh?"

"Did anybody hear him talking to you? Did anybody see him give you the note?"

"Nope. There wasn't nobody."

"You're sure? This is important, Dodo. Think. Think hard. Was anybody near?"

"There wasn't nobody. We was all alone. We was outside the pool room, down the bottom of the stairs in the hall, and there wasn't nobody around. You sure they'll gimme the ice cream sodas for the piece of paper?"

"Yes, they'll give you the sodas. Dodo, wasn't there anybody in the pool room—anybody at all?"

"No. There wasn't nobody."

"You're sure?"

"Sure I'm sure. I sweep up the place. There wasn't nobody in there."

"What about the man that runs the place? Wasn't he there?"

"He went to the bank. He didn't come back for a long time."

"And Jake Burdick just walked in there and gave you the note and went away?"

"Sure. He gimme a dime."

"All right. Now, after you got the note, did you show it to anybody?"

"No. I never showed it to nobody. I give it to you." He yawned. His eyes flickered and closed. Ed sat looking down at him for a minute or two and in that brief time Dodo was asleep again. Ed got up, turned off the light and went out.

IV

Several minutes later Ed found the pool room on Main Street. A sign, "Haggerty's Pool Parlor," creaked in the wind. Upstairs, the pool parlor was dark.

He got out of the car with his flashlight and crossed the sidewalk to the door of Haggerty's place. The pool room was on the second floor. The first floor was a grocery store. He tried the street door to Haggerty's. It was locked. He shone the light inside. There was a landing, a steep flight of stairs, and at the top a doorway labeled "Pool Room." Despite what the boy had said, could someone have been up there in the pool room, listening? Unless the talk between Dodo and Burdick had been in whispers, there was little doubt that someone might have heard.

"Looking for something?" The voice was quiet, suave, tinged with humor, but Ed leaped as if a cannon had gone off beside him. He whirled and shot the light full into the face of the dark figure beside him. It was the lawyer, Absalom Reynolds. "Looking for something?" Reynolds repeated, putting up a hand to shield his eyes from the light.

"Oh—you."

"Haggerty's closes at midnight," the lawyer offered. "It's almost one now." Ed shrugged and stepped down off the single stone step that separated Haggerty's door from the sidewalk.

"If I can help," Reynolds went on, "I'd be glad to."

"Sure," Ed grunted.

"I mean it. I hear Jacob Burdick was found murdered tonight."

"News gets around fast, doesn't it?"

"It does."

"I suppose you think I killed him, too, as well as Walt."

"Not at all. I don't think you killed anybody. I hope we aren't going to pick up where we left off last time."

Ed grunted.

"But of course you realize," Reynolds said, "that the two killings are connected."

"Are they? How?"

The lawyer shrugged. "They are in my mind, at least. Didn't you know that Walter Tuttle made his last several visits to Hamsted just to talk with Burdick?"

No, Ed hadn't known, but he said: "How does that connect their deaths?"

Reynolds shook his head. He drew the collar of his topcoat closer to his throat against the night wind. "I don't know how they're connected," he said, "but I do think they're connected. You see, I don't know what Tuttle came here to see Burdick about. I thought maybe you did."

Ed was looking away, down the street. "I don't," he said. "I didn't know there was such a person as Burdick till after Walt Tuttle was dead."

"He didn't leave any kind of communication," the lawyer suggested hesitantly, "that might give a clue?" Ed turned a bitter eye on the man. "If he left anything like that, he'd have left it with his attorney, wouldn't he? And you were his attorney, weren't you?"

"You're full of bitterness and grudges, aren't you?" Reynolds said softly. "Very well. Sorry I bothered you. Good night." He started away, then stopped and turned. "Oh, by the way, if you'll be in my office at three tomorrow, we'll read the will."

"Okay," said Ed.

The lawyer moved on and was swallowed up in darkness.

V

Binnie had her red mouth open to blast all hell out of Ed when he walked in at one-thirty. She shut it promptly, though, when she saw the light of excitement that burned in his eyes. He gave her a peck on the cheek and pushed her into an armchair.

"I think I've got something," he said, throwing his hat onto the console table and shedding his damp coat on the window seat.

"What?"

He lighted two cigarettes, gave her one, and began to walk the floor in quick strides. After several moments he halted, facing her. "Walt's murder isn't connected with Chicago. It's a Hamsted business all the way through."

"I'm listening."

He gave her the evening's crop.

"Walt's visits here were concerned with Burdick. Walt's dead, Burdick's dead. I think Walt knew something and Burdick knew the same thing, and both were murdered because of what they knew; Burdick because he was trying to get to me to tell me about it."

"Sure," said Binnie, blowing out a great cloud of smoke at him, "so that you'd be in on it and get murdered too."

He ignored this. "I'm going through Walt's things," he de-clared. "Every last scrap. Binnie, there *must* be a clue some-where." He saw her look of disapproval. "Binnie, I've *got* to find out what there is to find out. I can't let this go, I can't neglect it. I owe it to Walt; we both do."

"Okay," said Binnie gloomily. "There was a nice unused lot right next to where they laid Walt. It'll be just big enough for the two of us."

"Don't talk like that! Do you really want this thing to stop here? Do you, Binnie, do you?"

Their eyes met. She pressed out her cigarette in the ash tray on the arm of her chair, then got up. "Okay," she said, "let's go upstairs and start looking."

9
SOMEBODY IMPORTANT IN TOWN

I

Walt had eight trunks. There was a mountain of scripts, script notes, letters, Hollywood and Chicago publicity clippings, contracts and miscellany.

For two hour they sifted the mass. At a quarter to four they found something. It was an envelope labeled in Walt's hand: "Calla Forsythe." It was unsealed and in it were several clippings, most of them marked "Hamsted Courier," a few of them from Boston papers. The top of the batch was a *Courier* clipping.

CALLA FORSYTHE MURDERED
HAMSTED GIRL STRANGLED
IN HAMSTED WOODS

Pretty Calla Forsythe, 19, of Brenner Road North, was found dead on Thursday last in the Dennish Thicket of Hamsted Wood. She had been strangled by a person unknown and had been dead several hours. The body was found by Luigi Martinelli, A wood chopper, who was returning home in the late afternoon. Martinelli reported the matter at once to Chief of Police Albert Tomlin, who, with state police officers, went to the scene of the crime. It was determined that the girl had been strangled in the clearing beside the Dennish Thicket and then dragged out of sight into the heavy brush. It was

by the merest chance that Martinelli found her
when he stumbled over a twisted vine and fell into
the underbrush, his hand touching the girl's shoe.

While there is as yet no definite suspect, several
persons, whose names have not been made public,
have been questioned by the police. It is not known
that the girl had any enemies. Her family, which
consists of her mother, father and two brothers, is
at a loss to say who the murderer might have been.
They join in the general belief that the girl had no
enemies and are of the opinion that their daughter
was murdered by some stranger bent on assault,
although no sign of attempted criminal assault has
been admitted by the police. Funeral will be today
at ten a.m. from the Yoker Funeral Parlor.

The other clippings added little more than was contained in
this first one. The mystery of Calla Forsythe's death had gone
unsolved.

But there was something written on the reverse side of the
first clipping. It was penciled in Walt's bad scrawl, but it was
plain enough to read. It said, "Jacob Burdick"—and the name
was underlined.

They were seated on the floor reading the clippings. Finally
Ed sat back against the wall, the first clipping in his hand.

"Well?" Binnie asked.

"I've got to see Tomlin about this right away."

"Not *right* away," said Binnie. "Right away you're going to
bed."

"But I ought to—"

"It'll wait till tomorrow, or today, or whatever it is. If you're
one tenth as tired as I am, you're half dead, and you're going to
bed."

Ed yawned and pushed a hand through his thin, rumpled
hair. "Okay. I'm half dead all right. This clipping is three years
old. If it could wait this long, I guess it can wait a few hours
longer."

II

Ed walked into the chief's office and sat down while the chief finished talking on the phone. When he hung up he turned to Ed. "Want to see me?" Ed nodded. "'What about?"

"Well, first of all, what's my status today?"

The chief shrugged.

"Is that man supposed to be still on my tail? I haven't seen him."

The chief merely shrugged again.

"Anything new on Burdick's death?"

"Not a thing."

"I suppose you aren't in a mood to answer a few questions—or are you?"

"Depends on the questions."

"It's nothing that isn't public property. Do you mind telling me when you had your last murder in this town before—before Walt Tuttle?"

The chief eyed him quizzically for several seconds before answering, then said: "The last murder we had was a girl. Calla Forsythe. A nineteen-year-old girl. Why?"

"I don't know yet. Did you ever find out who did it?"

The chief shook his head. "Why do you ask about that?"

"I don't know yet," Ed repeated. "Will you tell me if you had any suspects?"

"Why?"

"Because," said Ed, leaning forward in his chair, "I want to know if that girl's death had anything to do with Walt's death."

"Why should it?"

"I don't know. I just wondered."

"Got a reason for wondering?"

"A reason, yes, but maybe not a very good one. I found some clippings in Walt's trunk, clippings about the girl's death."

"Are you trying to suggest," the chief said, examining his fingernails casually, "that Tuttle killed the girl and that somebody got back at him for that?"

"You know I'm not," Ed replied.

The chief examined one fingernail in particular. "It's an idea just the same, isn't it?"

"It's an idea," Ed agreed, "but it happens to be no good. You see, on the date of that girl's murder, Walt was producer of our radio show in Hollywood. It was a daily show and Walt never missed a day. You can check that as easy as pie. The sponsor was Bronson's Cakes and the advertising agency was McKechnie and Rounds, branch office in Hollywood. They'll tell you whether Walt was in Hollywood or elsewhere on that day."

Momentarily the chief flared up. "Then why the hell did you bring this whole damn thing up?"

"I told you I don't know yet," Ed replied. "Now will you answer my question about whether you had any suspects?"

The chief showed open, empty hands. "Our best guess was a tramp—a vagrant. But I'll be frank with you: We didn't have one guess that amounted to a hill of beans."

Ed pointed a finger at the chief as he got to his feet.

"Just as in Walt's case," he said. "Okay, Chief, I'll be seeing you."

III

The farmhouse was set back from the road about a hundred yards. Three big mongrel dogs, locked in a run, began to bark viciously as Ed drove in, past a silo, a chicken house and a tool shed, and pulled up at the front door. Binnie was with him, not because he wanted her with him or because he thought it was wise to have her but because she had threatened to go looking for a murderer by herself if she couldn't go looking with Ed. And since there was no knowing what kind of mischief she might get into on her own, he had taken her along.

He got out of the car. "You stay here," he warned. "And I mean right where you are; get it?"

"Yes, mister."

He walked slowly up the steps and knocked at the screen door. There was a murmur of men's voices from inside, and a woman's too, then the sound of a chair pushed back and footsteps approaching, footsteps that were heavy and slow.

A tall, gaunt old man, probably six feet tall, with stooped shoulders, came down the hallway. His gray-white hair fell in a lock over the right eye. There was a blue and white napkin tucked into the front of his work shirt. He pushed open the screen door and stepped out.

"Hello," Ed began. "Are you Mr. Forsythe?"

The old man looked at him steadily for a few seconds—the eyes were blue and hard—then his head turned a little and his gaze became fixed on Binnie in the car.

"My name's MacIntyre," Ed went on.

"What do you want?" The speech was slow. His eyes were still on Binnie. Somewhere in the distance a noon whistle blew.

"I wanted to talk with you—"

"About what? What do you want?"

"If you don't mind," Ed went on, "I want to talk with you about your daughter—your daughter Calla."

The thin, hard lips tightened; the eyes narrowed, fixed themselves on Ed and held there as he called:

"Johnnie! Gregg! Johnnie!"

Johnnie and Gregg came on the double at the urgency in the old man's voice. Johnnie was as tall as the old man and looked like a young edition of him, an unruly jet of black hair falling in the same manner over his right eye. Gregg was shorter and red-headed and built like an ape.

"What's the matter?"

Johnnie stood with his back to the screen door; Gregg stood slightly to one side, looking as if he were ready to leap.

The old man lifted a finger toward Ed. "He wants to talk to us about Calla."

Johnnie remained motionless. Gregg straightened a little.

"What does he want about Calla?" asked Johnnie.

There was something in the air that Ed did not understand. It was a hunch more than anything else that made him turn away with a little shrug. "There's no need to be hostile," he said. "I guess you don't want to talk. Sorry to bother you."

But before he could make a further move toward the steps, Johnnie said sharply: "Just a minute!"

Ed faced him again. Johnnie's hands were flat back against the screen door, down close to his sides. Gregg was looking not at Ed but from Johnnie to his father, his big head going back and forth slowly.

Johnnie said: "What about Calla?"

Ed shrugged again. "I don't know," he said. "I thought there wouldn't be any harm in coming to talk with you about her."

"Who are you? Why do you want to talk about her?" It was the old man this time, and as he spoke his thin, bloodless lips seemed barely to move.

"My name," Ed explained for the benefit of Johnnie and Gregg, "is MacIntyre. I live in town. I've been here about a week. I came here with my friend Walter Tuttle—"

Johnnie gave a little start. The redhead flushed to the roots of his hair. The old man didn't flick an eyelash. "Go on," he said as Ed paused.

"Walt was murdered," Ed said, looking at each of them in turn, "by a person or persons unknown."

Johnnie's chin came up a little. "Why tell us?"

Ed went on as if he had not interrupted. "I've just been through some of Walt's things. I found a bunch of newspaper clippings about the death of Calla Forsythe."

The redhead began to mumble low-voiced curses. "Shut up, Gregg," the old man ordered. His eyes went back to Ed. "Go ahead."

"I'd like to know if you can tell me why Walt saved those clippings."

"How the hell should *we* know!" Johnnie flung out.

"Take it easy, Johnnie," the old man cautioned. "Look, mister; get this and get it straight. We don't know anything about why anybody had any clippings anywhere. We don't know anything about—"

The redhead broke in savagely: "Ah, what the hell! What's the good of goin' about it this way!"

"Shut up, Gregg!"

"No, I won't shut up! Tuttle killed my sister—see? He was the one that murdered her! He did it and nobody else. We've known about that all the time. *That's* why he had them clippings—"

"*Shut up, Gregg!*"

Ed put in quietly: "If you think Walt did it—if you thought Walt did it, why didn't you tell the police?"

The redhead fumbled for words, then resorted to cursing again.

"What makes you think he did it?" Ed persisted.

"Shut up, Gregg'," said the old man, and the cursing stopped.

"Suppose I tell you something," Ed went on. "I don't know what you base your suspicion on, but I'll let you in on a little information. At the time your sister was murdered, Walter Tuttle was in California. I was there with him. I can prove where he was. Now if you want to tell me what you base your suspicion on—"

Johnnie cut in: "We don't want to tell you nothin'. All we want is for you and everybody else to mind your own business. Calla's dead. That's our business. That's our trouble, nobody else's. We don't want no buttin' in from you nor anybody else. Now, get outa here!"

"Wait a minute," the old man put in, almost with a soothing note in his voice. "Look, mister. This is a pretty touchy subject with us. We lost our little girl. The boys is pretty touchy about it, but they don't mean to be rough. Sometimes they can't help themselves; that's why they talk the way they did. Sometimes it ain't easy to speak nice when it's somethin' touchy you're talkin' about."

Ed was nodding slowly. "That's right," he said. "I understand exactly what you mean. I loved Walt Tuttle, probably almost as much as you loved your little girl. Okay. If that's all you have to say, let it go at that."

He turned then and went down the steps. He walked to the car and got in, conscious that their eyes were fixed on his back. He trod on the starter, swung the car around and drove out to the highway.

"Did you get that?" he asked Binnie.

Binnie was studying something over her open handbag. "What?" she asked in a preoccupied way.

"Could you hear what went on?"

"Every word, Ed."

"They think Walt killed the girl." Ed sniffed scornfully.

Binnie studied an old shabby little notebook. There was a calendar at the front of it, a calendar three years old.

"Ed."

"What?"

"Ed, I'm a stinker for saying this, I know. You've been saying that Walt was in California on the day the girl was murdered."

"Sure, and I—"

"Ed, the date she was murdered was a Sunday. Walt could have flown here after the Saturday show and he could have got back in time for the Monday show."

Ed swung the car over to the side of the road and brought it to a stop with a jerk. "Let me see that calendar," he said, and snatched it out of Binnie's hands. He studied it for a full minute, then looked away across the farmland that sprawled and undulated before them.

"Am I right?" Binnie asked.

Ed put the notebook in his pocket. "It doesn't prove anything," he said quietly. "Not a single solitary goddam thing." He paused. "But something did get proved just now. Those monkeys are holding something back. What it is I don't know, and what it's worth I don't know, but, by golly, I'm going to find out or I'll know the reason why."

IV

Paul Hastings was sitting at his desk when Ed walked into the untidy office of *The Courier*. Hastings was up to his shoulders in stacks of papers. He was in his shirtsleeves but his hat was on his head, tilted far back; there was a half-inch of cigarette in the corner of his mouth and he squinted at his work through blue smoke. There was a girl working at a typewriter in the corner diagonally opposite the door through which Ed had entered. She looked up over tortoise shell glasses and said: "Mr. Hastings."

Hastings looked at her, then turned his head to Ed. He pushed back his chair. "Hello, Ed." He kicked another chair around into place beside the desk and motioned Ed into it; snapped the end of a cigarette out of a pack and offered it to Ed; put his feet up on the stack of papers on the sliding panel of his desk and took a final drag on his cigarette. With one hand he ground the cigarette to death, with the other he handed Ed a sheaf of typewritten papers.

"There's your life in Hollywood," he said, exhaling a stream of smoke, "ready for the next issue." And then, as Ed took the papers but did not so much as glance at them, he went on: "What's on your mind, Ed?"

Ed reached into his coat pocket and took out the clippings on the death of Calla Forsythe. He handed them to Hastings. "Paul, can you give me any dope on this case?"

Hastings took the clippings and glanced through them briefly with a scowl. He shrugged. "I wrote those local bits," he said. "Everything I know is right there." He nodded slowly. "I remember the case only too well. As a matter of fact, it was my honeymoon." And as Ed found that puzzling, he went on: "The damned case broke the day before my wedding and we had to put off the ceremony so I could stay on and write the damn thing."

"What about the family, Paul—the Forsythes?"

Hastings shrugged. "Tight and bitter. That's about all you can say."

"That says it well enough. Tight about what they know. I think they know something they aren't telling."

Hastings looked at him steadily. "I don't get this," he said. "What's all this got to do with you?"

Ed shook his head. "I don't know—yet. I found the clippings in Walt's trunk. I thought I could get something out of the family. Paul, do you remember seeing Walt here at the time the girl was murdered?"

"No, I don't. Why?"

"Paul, I'm trying to cleanse my mind of the rotten suspicion the Forsythe clan planted. They suggest that Walt killed the girl." He drew a deep breath. "Tell me, Paul: There wouldn't be a picture of the girl here, would there? I'd like to know what she looked like."

"I think we have one." Hastings got up, went to a filing case in a corner, took out a folder, fingered through a number of photographs and finally handed one to Ed. "There she is."

It was an eight by ten glossy print, evidently a copy of a studio portrait, made for newspaper purposes.

"I think we ran that in one of the issues," Hastings added.

Ed nodded, studying the picture. Calla Forsythe was lovely and shy; the directness of her gaze was tinged with that shyness. Her features were well formed; the nose sensitive, the lips full and slightly parted, the chin tender. The hair was blonde and long, parted in the middle, braided and brought to the top of the head in a simple coronet. Ed met her eyes with a probing stare. There was an aliveness in those eyes; they seemed almost to speak.

Ed looked up at Paul Hastings. "Did she have a boy friend?" he asked.

"Evidently not. Nothing came out about a boy friend."

"Where'd you get this picture? From the family?"

"No. They were tight and bitter then, too. We got a picture from a girl friend of hers and made a copy."

"Who was the girl friend, Paul?"

Hastings took the picture out of Ed's hand, turned it over and handed it back. Written there was: "Original of this copy the property of Gladys Cross, 28 Stone St., Hamsted."

Ed jotted down the name and address, and got up. "Thanks, Paul. I'll see if she has anything to offer."

"I don't know what it'll get you," Hastings said. "I talked with her—and got nothing."

"Well, it'll give me something to do. So long, Paul."

V

First he went home and got Binnie, because he wasn't sure he could handle the matter alone. It was just as well, because Gladys Cross sat down and began to cry as soon as he mentioned Calla Forsythe.

"Please," said Binnie, "don't cry. We're trying to help."

"But she was my best friend," Gladys moaned, "and she died so young. It was simply terrible!" And she went on in an agony of tears.

Ed floundered around for the right thing to say but couldn't find it, so Binnie carried on. "Gladys, wouldn't you like to help find out who killed her? Wouldn't you?"

Gladys looked up out of a soaked handkerchief. She was a homely girl with irregular teeth, too many large freckles and brown hair unbecomingly done in a shoulder-length bob. She stared wide-eyed at Binnie through her tears. "Of *course* I'd like to help find out who killed her—if I knew how."

"Then suppose you stop crying and answer a few questions. Will you?" Binnie gave her a reassuring pat on the shoulder and sat down beside her. Ed took a chair by the window. Gladys dried her eyes, folded her hands tightly in her lap and kept her eyes fixed on them.

"How long had you known Calla, Gladys?" Binnie asked.

"I knew her all my life. We went to school together from the very first. We were—we were almost sort of like sisters together."

"Then I suppose she confided in you—told you all her little intimate secrets."

A little frown crossed Gladys' forehead like a small dark cloud. "N-no. She wasn't like that. Of course she told me lots of things, but I know there were lots of other things she didn't tell me."

Ed cleared his throat. "Do you know whether she was acquainted with Walter Tuttle, the man who was murdered in the drug store a few days ago?"

Gladys looked at Ed and nodded. "She knew him. She knew him from way back when she was a little girl."

"How old was she when she first met him?"

"Oh, maybe five or six. When we came down street together Mr. Tuttle used to buy us ice cream. He used to buy it for me only because I was with Calla. He never bought it for me when I was alone."

"That was how many years ago?"

"Well, it was about—about twelve years before Calla was—before she died. And she—she died three years ago."

Fifteen years. Walt would have been twenty-five at the time.

"And when she grew up—as she grew up, was Mr. Tuttle nice to her all along?"

The thin fingers twisted the wet handkerchief. "Whenever he was here. He went away more than ten years ago to go to Hollywood where he got famous."

"And he came back now and then to see Calla?"

"N-no, not to see Calla. I guess he just came back because it was his home here. He came back a couple of times when his aunt and his uncle died. And then a couple of times on vacation. And when he was here we'd see him downtown and he would treat us to an ice cream soda."

"Did he ever write to her; did she ever write to him?"

"I don't think so. I guess he sometimes sent her a Christmas card and she sent him one back, but I don't think he really ever wrote to her."

"Would you know," Binnie put in, with a glance at Ed, "if he was here in town around the time she was murdered?"

For a moment it looked as though Gladys were going to cry again, but she bit her lip to hold back the tears and said after a little pause: "I don't think he was here. I didn't see him. And Calla didn't say she saw him."

Ed drew a breath of relief, but then Gladys marred that relief. "Of course," she went on, "maybe he was here, and I didn't know it. For almost a year before Calla died I wasn't here in town much. I was working at a job over in Greenway and I was staying over there with my aunt and I didn't get back to Hamsted very often. I think she fell in love with somebody while I was away, though."

"Is that so?" Binnie asked quietly. "Who was it?"

Gladys frowned again. "I don't know. That was one of the things she wouldn't talk about."

"She wouldn't talk about someone she was in love with?" Binnie said. "Why not?"

"I don't know. I told you she was funny that way. All I ever got out of her was that it was somebody—somebody important in town."

"Important how?" Ed asked quickly, snatching at the clue.

She shook her head. "I don't know. I never found out. And then I think she must have broken up with him, because she went up to Boston to stay with her aunt all of a sudden. And I always thought she went away to forget."

"Just when did she go to Boston?" Ed asked.

"Let's see. I went to Greenway in October the year before she died. She went up to Boston the next January or February; I don't remember exactly."

"How long did she stay?"

"I don't remember for sure. Six or seven months, I think."

"Did you write to each other?"

"N-no. Calla wasn't very good at writing. She didn't like to write letters."

"Who is this aunt in Boston? Do you know her name? Do you know where she lives?"

"I've got it written down somewhere, I think." She got up and went to a Governor Winthrop desk and rummaged through a mass of papers. "Here it is. Mrs. Lottie Bramble. Here's the address here." She handed Ed a piece of crumpled paper.

VI

Binnie packed a bag while Ed sat on the edge of the bed and watched. He made a copy of Lottie Bramble's address in Boston and tucked it into the bag.

"You have a nice little heart-to-heart talk with Aunt Lottie," he said.

"You ought to come along too," Binnie grumbled. "You know I don't like going places alone."

"This isn't going places," Ed told her. "If I went, one of Tomlin's bloodhounds would be on my heels, and I don't want us annoyed until we've squeezed the good out of this thing."

"Yes, but what kind of good are we trying to squeeze out?"

"Use your very small but bright brain," Ed advised. "Ask Lottie everything you think of. Chiefly we want to find out who the boy friend was that Calla was in love with and broke up with and went to Boston to get away from and forget."

"Oke," said Binnie. Ed took her bag downstairs and tossed it into the back of the sedan and kissed Binnie as she sat behind the wheel.

"Bring back the liver and bacon," he said, "and don't get into trouble."

"What trouble?" Binnie asked. "Are you trying to scare me?"

"Not at all. Now beat it. And call me up just as soon as you get something."

"I will. Good-bye, sweet."

And she backed the car out like a stone from a sling.

VII

She phoned him from Boston the next afternoon. "We're in luck," she said. "Lottie runs a rooming house. I've got one of the rooms and Lottie's got a tongue hitched to a windmill in a gale. I haven't led up to Calla yet, but I will tomorrow."

"Keep shootin', toots," he said. "And be a good girl."

"You too, sweet. 'Bye."

VIII

She phoned again the next night.

"What's cooking?" he asked.

"More than you bargained for, my friend. If this is what I think it is, Ed, it's a stick of dynamite."

"What kind of dynamite?"

"I'll tell you tomorrow, when I get more dope."

"You tell me right now!" he ordered. "What have you got? Come on. Spill it."

"Let me pin it together first. I'll tell you tomorrow."

"I can pin it together!" he declared hotly. "Come on, give."

"Cheese it," she said. "Here comes Aunt Lottie. I've got to man the pump. Goodbye."

IX

He lived on pins and needles the next day. She didn't telephone again. Instead, she streaked into the garage, slammed on the brakes, and ran out of the garage to meet Mike the shepherd and Ed who followed Mike.

"I got it!" she said, and kissed him and dragged him inside the house. "Ed, what do you think of this: Calla Forsythe had an illegitimate baby in the Bruno Hospital in Boston in August, three months before she was murdered." Ed whistled softly. "Lottie gave out with a few leads and I followed them. Calla went to Lottie's for temporary shelter, then she went to the Bruno Hospital to have the child, and she came back here a month after the child was born."

Ed stared at her. "I don't get it. No one here seems to know anything about any child "

"Not even the Forsythes?"

Ed went for his hat and coat. "I'm going to find out," he said. "Right now."

10
DIG

I

The dogs were barking again when Ed rolled up the driveway of the Forsythe farm and came to a stop before the front steps, and this time they were loose. In, the moonlight they came charging at the car, one in front and one on each side, and leaped savagely at the doors. Ed calmly closed the window beside the driver's seat, sounded the horn once and waited.

He got action in thirty seconds. The front door opened and Johnnie Forsythe came out. "Who is it? Who's that?" he bellowed over the noise of the dogs. The dogs went on, crescendo. "Shut up, you goddam wolves! *Shut up!*" He stooped quickly and heaved something at the dog in front of the car. It was a chunk of wood and it caught the animal in the loin; the dog howled with fright and pain and darted away into the darkness, and the other two followed.

"All right," Johnnie called, "now who is it?" He came off the porch and walked to the car.

Ed rolled down the window. Johnnie peered, stared, recognized Ed and cursed softly. "Now look," he said, "I thought I told you to get the hell off this land and stay off."

"That's right," Ed nodded. "But something else has come up that I want to talk about, and I think you gentlemen"—he smiled faintly—"would like to talk about it too. In fact, I know you would." And he smiled again. The smile was what disturbed Johnnie.

"What?" he demanded.

121

"I'll talk to all three of you, inside," said Ed.

Johnnie suddenly came a step closer and his attitude was menacing. "About what?" he asked again.

"Something," Ed replied, "that I'm sure you'd rather have me talk with you about—than with the chief of police."

Johnnie's face hardened. "What're you givin' me?" he asked warily.

"Just invite me inside and I'll tell you."

As Johnnie hesitated, there was a sound at the front door of the house. Johnnie looked back over his shoulder. Forsythe Senior was standing behind the screen door, only barely visible in the shadows. "Tell him to come inside, Johnnie," the old man said quietly.

"Okay." Johnnie stepped back. Ed turned out the light, got out of the car, slammed the door and walked past Johnnie up the steps onto the porch where old man Forsythe held the screen door open.

"This is service," Ed thought. "I wonder what kind of jackpot I've hit."

Johnnie was close behind. The old man moved ahead into a room on the right where a table lamp gleamed dully. "Sit down." The old man pointed to a straight-backed chair beside the table that bore the lamp.

"I'll sit here, thanks," Ed said, deliberately choosing the chair nearest the door through which they had entered.

"Suit yourself." He raised his voice. "Gregg! Gregg, come on down here! Come on down here right away!"

Muffled by walls and distance, Gregg's voice came back. "Comin! I'm comin'."

In a moment he came thundering down steps and strode into the room and past Ed before he saw him. "Hello, Gregg," Ed said.

Gregg halted, turned sharply and glared down at him. Then he looked from Johnnie to his father. "I thought we told him—"

"Sure," the father cut in quietly. "We told him. Now he's back again."

"Persistent kind of feller, ain't he?" Gregg sneered. "You want I should throw him out for the dogs?"

"Don't throw nobody," the old man went on. "He's got some-thin' to say—somethin' he wants to say to us better than to the chief of police."

Gregg's glance was locked for a moment with his father's; then it turned once more upon Ed and there was in it a new light, a light this time of wariness, the wariness of a sullen an-imal. He backed off from Ed and there was a threat even in his retreat, as if he were measuring the distance for a spring.

"What's he want to say to us better than to the chief of police? Huh?"

"Ask him."

Gregg had not taken his eyes off Ed. Now, his retreat halted, he came a step closer and pointed a blunt red finger.

"You get the hell out of here," he said. "You can go on and tell twenty-eight goddam chiefs of police any goddam thing you know about us. We never done nothing to tell nobody about and I don't know what you asked him inside for."

"Maybe," said the old man softly, "he wants to tell about the time you stole apples over at Percher's."

"Guess again," said Ed, just as softly.

"Let's beat him up," Gregg suggested. "He ain't got no wit-nesses—"

"The best witness you can give me," Ed pointed out, "is just one black eye. Go ahead, beat me up. You can do it. It's three to one. Then the chief of police will ask me why you did it and I'll tell him—"

"Suppose everybody shuts up," put in Johnnie, "and see what kind of tripe he's got to tell us. That's what we brought him in for. Okay, brother, suppose you say your little piece."

Ed nodded. "Okay, I'll say my little piece, brother. But first of all let me tell you this: I'm not looking for trouble. Far from it. If trouble happens to come along with what I'm looking for—well, so be it. I happen to be looking for the person or persons who murdered my friend Walter Tuttle. And take my word for it, brothers"—he looked about at, all three of them—"I shall say or do whatever is necessary at any time to find out what I need to find out. Every time I run into something that looks suspicious,

I intend to yank it up by the stalk and see what makes it grow. And I'm about to do a little yanking right now, if you've got guts enough to let me go ahead with it."

"We're listenin', ain't we?" Johnnie pointed out.

"Okay," said Ed. "Now, I happen to know for an absolute dead certainty—so you needn't scream me down denying it—I happen to know for an absolute dead certainty that your sister Calla had an illegitimate child—"

Gregg came for him like a tiger. One big paw swiped savagely in a sidewise blow and knocked Ed off the chair and sprawling on the floor. The old man grabbed Gregg and held him off. Ed got up and slammed a fist into Gregg's face before Johnnie grabbed him, jerked him back into his chair and held him there by the back of his coat collar.

"That's enough," the old man warned. "Let him finish his story before you kill him. I'd like to know jest exactly how much else he's made up and how much else we'll have to give the lie to. Go ahead, mister—keep on talkin'."

But there was another interruption. There was a vague sound in the hallway, a tread of soft footsteps, and Ed turned to see a gray-haired, stoop-shouldered woman standing there. She would have said something, but Johnnie, releasing his hold on Ed, moved quickly to block the doorway.

"You go on upstairs, Ma," he said. "Go ahead, Ma. This ain't none of your business, now."

She looked past Johnnie and the eyes she fixed on Ed were filled with a strange anxiety.

"I don't want no fightin'," she said in a tired voice. Her eyes shifted. "I don't want no fightin', Pa."

"There won't be no fightin'," the old man promised.

"Gregg, you hear me? I don't want no fightin'."

Gregg only glared sullenly. The old man let go of him and said: "There won't be no more fightin'. Don't worry, M. Go on upstairs."

The woman went away, shaking her head slowly. Johnnie closed the door and stood with his back to it. "All right," he said to Ed. "You can go on now."

"Okay," Ed said. "Right where we left off. I'm going to repeat what I said and I don't want to get knocked on my face for it. I'm repeating now—and I'm not saying it to hurt your feelings. I'm just giving you cold facts that I can prove. There was a child; there is a child somewhere. Where, I don't know; maybe you don't either. I'm just telling you facts as they are."

"Those facts being just what?" old man Forsythe asked.

"Just this: Your daughter had a child in the Bruno Hospital in Boston three months before she was murdered. Hold it, Gregg; I can prove every word. Now, in my opinion that child had something to do with her death; it's my theory that the father of that child murdered your daughter, most likely so that she wouldn't talk."

Gregg went to the door, opened it and said quietly:

"Get your goddam theories outa here. We ain't listening to no more dirty talk about my kid sister. Now get outa here."

Ed looked at the father and then at Johnnie. Their faces were grim, their eyes hard. Ed shrugged. "Okay. Have it your own way."

He walked through the doorway as casually as he could, went down the hall, opened the outer door, and turned back for a last glance. Only Gregg stood there.

"I'd appreciate an escort through that pack of dogs," Ed said.

"Go to hell," said Gregg, but Johnnie stepped out of the parlor and came to join Ed. They went out without a word, and down the steps to the car. The dogs were quiet and kept their distance. Ed got into his car, said good night to Johnnie, swung the car around and drove off.

He had driven perhaps half a mile from the Forsythe place when he heard a sound in the back seat of the car. Startled, Ed swung the car to the side of the road and brought it to a quick stop.

II

"What are you doing here? How'd you get here?"

It was Dodo Brown. He sat placidly in the back seat, his hands folded in his lap, his little eyes gleaming in the light from the dashboard.

"I heard," he said.

Ed eyed him silently for several seconds. Then: "You heard what?"

"I saw too," Dodo went on.

"What did you see? What are you talking about?"

"I seen everything. In the house. I was outside. Lookin' under the shade. Shades wasn't down all the way."

"What were you doing there? How'd you happen to go there?"

The boy's grin widened. "I go there sometimes," he declared.

"Where do you mean? To the Forsythe farm?"

The big head nodded placidly.

"What do you go for? What business have you got up there?"

Dodo shrugged. "I just go."

"So you were outside the window looking and listening? And then you got into my car?"

The boy nodded. "When I saw you was comin' out."

Ed turned on the ceiling light of the car and contemplated Dodo. The boy wore a cap pulled down over one eye.

"There are three dogs up there," Ed said. "Why didn't they bark when you were outside that window?"

"They know me. They don't bark when I come."

"Why'd you go up there tonight, Dodo?"

The boy shrugged again. "I dunno."

"You just went up there for the fun of it? Or were you following me up there?"

The smile, which had receded, now lifted the lips again. "I can run fast," Dodo pointed out, "but not fast enough to follow a car. You came in a car."

"You weren't by any chance in the back of the car, right where you are now, when I drove up?"

The big head shook emphatically. "No. No, Mr. MacIntyre. I didn't know you was coming."

"You must have had some reason for going up there, Dodo. Come on. Tell me about it."

The boy's eyes rolled and shifted from side to side, in an exaggerated, melodramatic display of caution.

"Certainly you must want to talk about it," Ed pressed him, "or you wouldn't have got into my car, Dodo."

The boy shook his head. "My name ain't Dodo," he declared with a new dignity. "People make fun of me, call me Dodo. Dodo, that's a name for a fool."

"Alright. What is your name?"

"My name's Will."

"All right, Will. I'd have called you that before, only I didn't know."

The boy nodded thoughtfully. "No, you didn't know," he agreed.

"How about it?" Ed urged. "Come on, Will: What did you go up to the Forsythe farm for?"

The big head shook again. "I won't tell. But I'll show you."

"All right. What are you going to show me?"

"First we got to go somewhere."

"Where?"

"We got to go somewhere and get some shovels."

Ed sat upright. A horrible chill went up and down his spine. "What for? Are we going to dig for something? What is it, Will? What are we going to dig for?"

"I'll show you," said Will. "First we go get the shovels."

III

There was no coaxing Dodo Brown. He would talk or not talk, as his mood required, and now he stared into the dark of the roadside and ignored Ed, who tried several times to start him talking. Finally Ed pulled up in front of the house, got out and went around back and down into the cellar to explore for shovels. Mike began to bark at once. Exploring by matchlight, Ed stumbled over several odds and ends and made enough noise so that after a few minutes a door opened somewhere above and Binnie called out urgently:

"Who is it? Who's down there?"

"It's only me," Ed hollered back.

"It's a good thing," she said. "I was just going to sick Mike down there. What are you doing?"

"Looking for something."

"Looking for what?"

"Don't ask so many questions. I'll tell you later."

"Okay," she called. "Are you coming upstairs soon?"

"No. I'm going out again."

"Where?"

"No place in particular."

"We-el—well, okay, but don't stay out too late."

"Okay, okay." And he saw what he was looking for: a pair of shovels, standing in a corner beside the furnace. He picked them up and hurried out of the cellar and back to the car. Dodo had moved up to the front seat. Ed put the shovels in the back of the car and got in behind the wheel.

"All right, now; where to?"

"The Forsythe farm."

"You mean back where we came from?"

The boy nodded.

IV

As they approached the entrance to the Forsythe farm, Dodo Brown pointed ahead. "Don't go in there. Go on down the road."

The road swung to the right, a neglected road, rutted and pocked and planted with boulders. The land beyond the headlights was black as ebony, for only a sliver of moon rode in murky clouds. To the left was open, unfenced country. On the right the Forsythe farm was hemmed with a log fence. They had driven for perhaps a quarter of a mile when the boy leaned forward and pointed.

"Stop there," he said. "That's the best place."

Ed swung left into a little grove of trees and kept the car moving until it was out of sight of anyone passing on the road. Then he stopped, yanked up the parking brake, turned out the lights and sat back. "Now what?"

"Now we go—back there." A big thumb jerked over his shoulder.

"All right. Lead the way."

They got out. Ed reached into the back of the car and took out the shovels. The big flashlight that was clamped to the steering post he shoved into his coat pocket. He gave one shovel to Dodo, shouldered the other one himself and followed the boy, who went briskly off as if he could see as well by night as by day, his slight limp in no way interfering with his quick stride.

They crossed the road and came to the log fence. The boy climbed over and went on without even turning to see if Ed was still with him. His pace was quickening now; Ed lengthened his stride to come up alongside.

He said in a whisper: "Don't you think you'd better tell me what we're going to do—what we're going for?"

"We're gonna dig," the boy replied. "You'll see."

The ground was flat and uncultivated and it seemed to lead nowhere except into the darkness. They walked several hundred yards before Ed made out a towering thicket of trees against the dim gold of the moon. He could smell pine and soon felt the soft cushioning of the needles underfoot. They went through the thicket and out of it onto open land again, this time a narrow stretch, and once again into a patch of pines. Here the boy halted and stood silent for several moments. Ed waited beside him. The boy spoke without turning his head. "It's here—somewhere."

"All right. Where?"

"I ain't sure. I thought I was sure, but I ain't."

"Tell me what we're looking for. Maybe I can spot it."

"I can find it."

"Here. Take the light."

Ed put the flashlight in his hand. The boy pressed the button and cast the light about him thoughtfully.

Then he limped away slowly, searching the ground with the light. Off in the distance a dog began to bark. The boy turned off the light, waited. Then in a few moments he turned it on again and went walking down through the thicket. Ed remained where he was, watching. *Either we're chasing bubbles or this guy's crazy as a fox*, he said to himself.

The boy turned around and came back. He said in a strange, worried, frustrated way:

"I knew where it was. But I can't find it now."

"Look," Ed told him, "if you'd tell me what we're looking for, maybe I could help you find it."

The boy turned away. "I can find it." But then he stiffened and stood still, and the light in his hands went out. . . . The barking of dogs . . . more than one dog this time. Through the trees Ed could see two lights bobbing and weaving, and coming toward them—fast.

"That's the Forsythes," Ed said quickly. "They've seen that light. I'm getting out of here. Come on!" But the boy stood rooted to the spot. Ed came up and took his arm. "I said let's get out of here. We can get back to the car. Come on!"

The boy shook off his hand. "You can't run faster than dogs."

"Brother, I can try. *Come on!*"

"No! I know what to do. Don't run. I can fool them. You go in the bushes—over there."

He gave Ed a yank and a push so hard that Ed almost fell on his face and went stumbling, shovel and all, toward a squat clump of bushes. The barking of the dogs was very near now. There was nothing to do but to continue to stumble into the heart of the brush. He fell on his face and elbowed his way around so that he could see what was about to happen.

It was already happening. The boy flung his shovel into another bush, turned on the flashlight and began to walk directly toward the approaching lights and dogs. He waved the flashlight and quickened his shuffling pace.

The dogs were on lead. They came charging at Dodo. The boy spoke a word of greeting and the barking ceased instantly, savagery changed to joy, and the dogs began to leap and vie for the boy's attention and affection. "Good dogs," said Dodo. "Good dogs. I came to see you. Good dogs!"

There was an oath from Gregg Forsythe. "You god-dam goon!" he yelled. "Did you get us out of the house on another of your visits! I ought to break you in six pieces!"

He lifted his hand savagely and the boy cowered away. Old man Forsythe broke in: "It's no good hittin' him, Gregg, you know that! Let him be!"

"What do, you mean, let him be! He gets us out of the house this time o' night, I ought to kill him!"

"Cut it out, Gregg." That was Johnnie. Johnnie stepped up to stand close, looking down at Dodo. "Now look, Dodo, we told you three times to be a good feller and stay off our land."

"I only like to come and talk to the dogs," Dodo insisted plaintively.

"Never mind what you like! We don't want you on the land here nights—you hear? If you want to come up to the house in the daytime and talk to the dogs, okay, but we don't want you nosin' around here in the night. You see this shotgun? It's lucky we didn't fill you full of holes, see?"

"I only like to come and talk to the dogs in the nighttime, when they're all alone," the boy said. "I didn't do nobody no hurt."

Gregg lunged forward. He flung the boy around and with a brutal kick sent him staggering away. The dogs began to growl.

"Now you get the hell outa here!" Gregg cried. "And stay out." He swung about to face the dogs. "And if you lousy mutts growl at me, I'll kick your teeth right down your throat. You hear me?"

"Cut it out, Gregg," said the old man. "None o' that, now."

"No? My own dogs sidin' with that halfwit ag'inst me! I'll kick 'em right in the neck!"

"Stop talkin' like that. You know well enough a dog always favors a halfwit."

"Sure. They got somethin' in common—they're both dumb. But just the same, don't you mutts ever show your teeth to me or I'll kill you!"

Ed saw Dodo fade like a shadow into larger, darker shadows. He lay still, wondering if the dogs would sense his presence. Flat on his stomach, he looked out through the bush, his eyes fixed on the three men and the dogs. Gregg was still stewing and cursing. Johnnie and the old man were silent and still, turned in the direction of the retreating Dodo.

Johnnie said: "What do you think, Pa? You think there's anything goin' on in that halfwit's head?"

"Don't talk like a fool," the old man said quietly. "Don't go imaginin' things."

"Just the same, I'm gonna go take a look."

"All right. Go take a look. I'll stay here and see he doesn't come back."

The old man held the lead of one of the dogs and Johnnie, who held the leads of the other two, handed them to his father. He picked up Gregg's lantern and started away in silence. He went past Ed's group of bushes, so close that Ed could have touched him on the way by. In a silence that was complete except for the crunching of pine needles underfoot, Johnnie went away to become only a bobbing and swinging light. Suddenly the light stopped moving, was still for perhaps half a minute; then it swung in a half-circle as Johnnie turned around, and came back at the same slow gait that had taken him on his errand.

"Everything's okay, Pa," he said. "Come on; let's go back to the house. Come on, Gregg."

They moved away in silence. Even the sullen Gregg had bottled up his cursing and he followed the other two, hands thrust in trousers pockets, head down.

"Keep going, gents," Ed said silently. "Much obliged and good riddance."

He waited several minutes, until the lanterns were pinpoints of light, then threw out his shovel and crawled out after it. He got to his feet and turned his nose straight for the spot that Johnnie had visited. There was a small glimmer of light from the moon, too small to do any good. Ed stumbled over a pine stump and fell headlong to the ground. The shovel clattered on wood and rang on stone and Ed lay still, wondering if in that enveloping silence the sound of his awkwardness had carried across the fields to the Forsythes. No Forsythe returned.

But Dodo Brown did. "Hsst!" the hiss preceded him by many seconds. "Hsst!" Then Ed heard the shuffle and crunch of the boy's step. "Hsst! Mister MacIntyre!"

"I'm over here," said Ed, getting up and nursing a knee.

"They're gone," Dodo announced.

"That's right." Dodo stood only a few steps away now. "Now look, my friend, let me tell you something: I think the job you did in handling the Forsythes was swell, and I give you a lot of credit. You fooled them four ways from Sunday. But now we're in sort of a bad spot, so I want to know what we came up here for. To dig, I know—but to dig what? Tell me and let's get it over with. Now, what is it?"

The answer came with less urging than Ed had expected to use. "There's a dead body—dead and buried—and *they* buried it. I seen 'em do it. All we got to do is find the right spot—the spot we were looking for before they came."

"I think I can find it," Ed said. He thumbed over his shoulder in the direction in which the Forsythes had vanished. "Johnnie Forsythe took a look at a spot right over there."

A pleased calculating grin spread slowly over Dodo's face. He had never looked quite so foolish nor spoken quite so wisely. "I kinda figgered maybe they would," he said. "That's why, when you give me the flashlight, I kept shinin' it down at the house—so they'd see."

This left Ed speechless and slightly sick for several seconds. "And what if they'd filled us full of lead?" he queried at last.

But Dodo ignored the question. He walked away from Ed, thrust head and shoulders into a bush and emerged with his discarded shovel. Ed picked up his own and started again for the spot Johnnie had singled out.

"I'm not sure just where it was," he said thoughtfully, "but it was pretty close by."

This was all the clue that Dodo needed. He went quickly past Ed, walked up to a giant pine, turned on the flashlight, smothering its light to a mere glow with his hands, and searched for something at the very base of the tree. "See!" he said triumphantly. "That's my mark!"

There was a horizontal gouge in the bark at ground level, a gouge three inches long and half an inch wide. It was dirt-stained and almost imperceptible. "They buried it here!" he declared dramatically, pointing to the spot on which Ed stood.

Ed moved aside. The boy turned off the flashlight, set it down, spat on his hands and began to shovel.

There were several inches of pine needles. "It's down deep," the boy said, and Ed began to shovel beside him. They struck soft earth and kept digging, deepening and widening the hole. There was only eagerness in the boy, but in Ed there was a slow-creeping horror, a horror akin to that which had strangled him as he had scraped the dirt from the mortal remains of Jacob Burdick.

Suddenly the hole was too deep to dig from above and the boy jumped into it. Ed leaned on his shovel, mopped his brow, and had wave after wave of nausea. Dodo shoveled frantically and the dirt flew. At length he threw out his shovel and began to scratch and scrape with his hands. Then Ed saw him up-end something and lift it up. In the poor light it looked like a wooden box. It was about three feet long and two feet wide.

Dodo handed it up to Ed. "This is it!" he declared with an unholy eagerness.

Ed leaned down and took it. It was light, weighing about fifteen pounds. Ed set it down on the ground and gave the boy a hand up.

Off in the distance the Forsythe dogs began to bark again. The boy snatched up the box, and Ed grabbed the two shovels. "Let's get out of here!"

They went at a trot through the pine thicket. A few minutes later they reached the car.

11

THE MISSING LETTER

I

They drove up to the police station and got out. Ed could see the light shining in the chief's office. Dodo, sitting in the back of the car with the box on his knees, handed it to Ed, who took it with a little grimace. "Come on," he said to Dodo, and turned and went into the station.

He walked down the corridor. The chief's outer office. was open and so was the inner. Ed could see Tomlin's big feet on his desk. Tomlin was talking to someone.

Ed went through the outer office and stopped in the doorway. Paul Hastings was sitting in a chair tilted back against the wall, facing the chief, his hat tilted on the back of his head. Hastings turned toward the door with a quizzical glance. Tomlin took his feet off the desk and, frowning, said: "What's that?"

Ed set it on the end of Tomlin's desk and dusted off his hands. "I don't know," he said. "It's all yours."

"What's in it?" Tomlin got up. He sniffed sourly, fixing a hard eye on the box, "Where'd you get it?"

"Dug it up. Dodo—I mean Will Brown and I—" He turned to indicate Dodo, but there was no Dodo. He looked at Tomlin again, puzzled. "I thought he came in with me."

"Who? That halfwit? What's he got to do with it? What's it all about?"

Ed shrugged. "The boy told me there was something buried out on the Forsythe place. We went up there just now and dug this up."

"And you don't know what it is?"

"Not for sure. I've got a pretty good guess."

The chief pulled open a desk drawer, took out a burglar's jimmy and a hammer. "And your guess is what?"

"Calla Forsythe had an illegitimate child." The chief's eyes bulged; Paul Hastings brought his tilted chair quietly to the floor and leaned forward in it, listening intently. Ed went on: "I think it's in there."

The chief went to work on the box. It was open in a few minutes. In it was a bundle wrapped in an old oilskin raincoat. The chief picked up the bundle and unrolled it carefully.

II

The state troopers' car, with five troopers, rode up the dark driveway of the Forsythe place. The chief's car followed. With the chief were Officer Brewer, Ed MacIntyre and Paul Hastings. They drove up in front of the farmhouse and the dogs were out to greet them in a flash. They lined up between the cars and the house and began a chorus of ferocity. The chief yelled above the din: "Stay in the car. Stay where you are, boys!"

A light went on in an upstairs room, a window shot up and old man Forsythe stuck out his head. "Who's down there? What do you want?"

The chief shouted back: "This is Chief Tomlin. We've come to get you and the boys. Now we want you to call off those dogs and come down nice and peaceable. You hear me?"

There was a brief, calculating pause. Then: "What for? What've we done?"

"I guess you know what you've done. Now call off the dogs before we put a flock of bullets in 'em, and come on down here like good fellers."

A big hand yanked the old man away from the window and Gregg took his place. "If we're such good fellers, what do you want us for? Shut up, Pa! Let me talk: What do you want us for, Tomlin?"

"Murder," said Tomlin. "Now are you comin' down or do we come up and get you?"

"Why, you lousy rat!" Gregg howled. "If you want us for murder, I'll give you a murder to pin on us!"

"Duck!" shouted one of the state troopers. "He's got a shotgun!" The shotgun blazed and roared. Slugs slammed against the car and bit their way into the roof of the car. The aim was too high. One of the troopers fired back. The bullet hit the window frame and shattered the glass and Gregg ducked out of sight. The dogs ducked too, scampering away into the darkness.

The troopers' car suddenly shot away down the drive and the chief's car followed. Gregg was hollering after them that they were dirty cowards, when the strategy of the retreat became apparent. The troopers' car turned off its lights and swung sharply left into the area enclosed by the driveway; the chief followed suit; the troopers lunged out of the car and made for the cover of several scattered trees. The chief, curtly ordering Ed and Hastings to stay where they were, joined the troopers at a run.

There was an interval of silence, perhaps ten seconds; then one of the troopers shouted out of the darkness: "Now look, you guys; we've got you covered with machine guns and gas guns and we're coming to get you. If you want to come out alive, okay. If you want to come out dead on a slab, that's okay too. Now which is it? Speak up!"

The answer was a shot from the now darkened house.

"Okay, let 'em have it!" the trooper shouted, and the machine guns began to blast. From the house came the bark and flash of three separate shotguns at different windows and the vicious shouting, incoherent now, of Gregg Forsythe.

Then, abruptly, a woman began to scream, and suddenly the front door opened and Mrs. Forsythe came running out and down the steps and across the driveway like a panic-stricken animal.

"Hold it!" Johnnie shrieked. "Hold off the firin'! It's Ma! Don't shoot! Don't shoot! Stop shootin'!"

The firing ceased on both sides and one of the troopers came out to meet the woman, who flung herself on her knees at his feet and begged him not to kill her men folks.

"That's okay with us, lady. You just tell 'em to throw their guns out the window and come down with their hands up in the air and nobody's gonna get killed." But the woman was in no condition to carry out orders coherently, so the trooper relayed them in a loud voice.

"All right!" Johnnie called back; then there was a brief pause before the guns came clattering down onto the driveway.

"Now come out with your hands up."

Half a minute later all three came marching out, single file, hands in the air. They descended the steps at a slow pace and the troopers closed in to meet them, tommy guns ready.

III

"You might as well come clean, men," Depew told the Forsythe father and sons. "Sitting there with your tongues tied isn't doing you any good at all. The situation looks pretty bad. Now, if you've got anything to explain, maybe it'll help you. If you want a lawyer, I'm offering you one again."

The Forsythe men sat side by side in Chief Tomlin's office, and Mrs. Forsythe sat hunched beside her husband, frozen in a stupor of grief. At last Forsythe Senior opened his hard, thin lips and spoke. "You let my wife go and we'll talk."

Depew, seated on a corner of Tomlin's desk, looked at Tomlin, who sat behind the desk. Tomlin shrugged a fraction of an inch. Ed MacIntyre, seated in a corner to the right of the chief, took out a package of cigarettes and handed them to Paul Hastings, who stood beside him making notes in a leather-covered notebook. Hastings took a cigarette, struck a match, held it first for Ed's cigarette, then his own, flicked the life out of the match and dropped it in the corner.

"Why should we let her go?" Depew asked. "She's in it just as deep as you are."

"No she ain't," the old man mumbled. "She don't know nothin' about it."

Depew glanced back at Tomlin again and they exchanged nods.

"Okay," Depew said, "we'll let her go. Send her home, Tomlin."

Tomlin got up and went to the door that led to the front corridor. He opened it. "Johnnie—Johnnie Brewer." Officer Brewer came down the corridor. "Take Mrs. Forsythe home," Tomlin directed.

Mrs. Forsythe got up unsteadily. Johnnie Brewer came forward and helped her. Tomlin closed the door behind them.

"All right," said Depew. "Now talk."

The old man did the talking. A few months before her death, Calla had given birth to a child, a girl. The birth had taken place in Boston, where they had sent her as soon as they realized what was going to happen. Following the birth of the child, she had returned to Hamsted. They had continued to conceal the fact that she had a child, and then Calla had been murdered. Three months later the child died suddenly. They buried it in the pine grove on their farm.

"What was wrong with the child?" Depew asked. "Why did it die?"

"It died of pneumony," the old man said. "That's what we thought it was."

"Why didn't you have a doctor?"

"Because we didn't think it was sick enough. It didn't seem bad, but then one morning we woke up and it was dead." His blunt, awkward fingers fumbled at each other with a strange nervous gesture.

"Didn't you know it was your duty to report the death and give the child proper burial?" The old man was silent and Depew pressed him: "Didn't you know that?"

Forsythe mumbled: "Calla was dead. We didn't want to bring no disgrace on her. That's the only reason we done it."

"Who was the father of the child?"

The rugged, slumped shoulders moved in a shrug. "We never found out. But we think we know who it was."

"And who do you think it was?"

Gregg Forsythe looked up sharply and his blue eyes shot fire at Ed MacIntyre. "We know damn well who it was! It was that sneakin', low-down friend of that guy over there. It was that guy Tuttle, the guy that got what was coming to him down in the drug store—that's who it was!"

"You're sure it was Tuttle?"

"Sure I'm sure!"

"What makes you sure? What evidence did you have?"

"Ah, he was always too damn interested in Calla. He wanted to send her to school—wanted to pay all the bills. Whenever he came to town she'd see him; we didn't know what they were doin' then, but we know now!"

"Just a minute," Ed broke in, getting to his feet. "Excuse me, Mr. Depew. I'd like to put in about two cents' worth for Walt Tuttle—"

"Not now," said Depew curtly, without taking his eyes off Gregg Forsythe. "So what you did, Gregg, to pay Tuttle back, was go down to the drug store and give him what was coming to him, eh?"

Gregg's lips curled in a cold sneer. "Ain't you smart! I don't know who gave Tuttle what was comin' to him, but I'd shake hands with him good if I did know."

Depew ignored the sneer. "Let's go back a step or two," he said. "I asked you if you knew who the father of Calla's child was and you gave me your guess about Tuttle. What I want to know is this: Didn't the girl confide in anyone; didn't her mother know?"

Forsythe Senior answered soberly: "She wouldn't confide in none of us, even her mother. Somehow she didn't talk much to us in a confidin' way. The only one she ever used to go confidin' to was Jake Burdick." Depew and Tomlin exchanged glances. "When she had some cryin' to do, she'd go down to Jake Burdick and do it. Jake was the only one she ever told anything," he finished sadly, and a single tear rolled down his cheek and splashed, glistening, on the back of his hand.

"Uh-huh. And now Burdick's dead. And it would seem Burdick was killed because he knew who killed Tuttle." Depew got to his feet, smoothed his bald dome with a single stroke and rubbed the back of his head in a frustrated way. "What a stinking tangled-up mess this case is!" He walked slowly to the water cooler in the corner behind the Forsythes, drew a paper cupful of water, gulped it, then said over his shoulder: "Lock them up, Tomlin. I'll talk with them again in the morning."

Gregg jumped to his feet. "There's only one other thing *I* got to talk about!" His hard eyes were fixed venomously on Ed. "When I get my mitts on the dirty rat that got us hauled down here, so help me I'll—"

"Shut up, Gregg," said Johnnie quietly. "All right, Tomlin, if you're gonna lock us up, go ahead and lock us up."

"Do you want a lawyer?" Tomlin asked once more.

"No," said Johnnie. "We can talk for ourselves."

"Suit yourself." Tomlin got up, opened the door that that led to a smaller office and the cell block. "Hey, Marcus, lock these men up. All right, you," he said to the Forsythe trio. "This way."

They filed out silently. Tomlin went back to his desk and sat down. He swiveled around in his chair to face Ed and Paul Hastings.

"You don't use any of this yet, Paul," he cautioned. "Not till I give the go-ahead."

"Okay," Hastings nodded. He flipped his notebook shut and slipped his pencil into his vest-pocket.

Tomlin leaned back in his swivel chair and stared thoughtfully at the ceiling. After a while he spoke. "What I want to know," he said, "is what's what with the dummy Dodo Brown." He clasped his hands behind his head. "I'd like to know just where he fits in this picture. He comes and he goes too often to suit me." He unclasped his hands and got up. "Well, if the mountain won't come to Mohammed, we'll go find the mountain." He reached for his hat. Ed MacIntyre got to his feet. The chief turned a sharp eye in Ed's direction, shaking his head. "Not you," he said. "You've been mixin' in too much where you ain't got any business. Suppose you be smart for once and go home and go to bed."

Ed said nothing. Hastings raised his eyebrows as if to ask whether he was invited. Tomlin shook his head. "We'll make this visit alone," he said.

IV

Tomlin took Johnnie Brewer's flashlight out of Johnnie's hand and shot the light up the wide dusty stairs. Slanting shadows scurried back from the white gleam, stood rigid for a moment, then rocked crazily back and forth as Tomlin swung the light to examine the whole corridor. There was nothing, no one, and the only sounds were the rumblings of sleep. Tomlin started up the squeaking stairs. Brewer took a look into the dark behind him, made a wry face at the stale corridor smells and followed the chief upstairs.

At the top of the steps Johnnie said: "Straight ahead. The end of the hall. On the right."

Tomlin went quickly down the hall, laid a hand on the knob of Dodo Brown's door and threw the door open. He stepped in, hesitated a moment, swung the beam of light about the room.

"Well, he ain't here," said Johnnie Brewer. He followed Tomlin into the room and closed the door behind him. Tomlin reached up and turned on the single naked bulb that swung from the ceiling. "What a dump," said Brewer.

Tomlin went to the table, pawed the few articles that lay on top of it: a half-eaten apple, a pencil stub, several buttons, an empty ink bottle, a much-gnawed penholder with a rusty pen-point, a wad of tangled, dirty gray string, some wooden matches, and a twisted, crumpled, dried out tube of glue. Tomlin yanked open the table drawer and found a similar miscellany. He went over the items quickly, flicking them from side to side with a long forefinger. Johnnie Brewer yawned. "What're we looking for?" he asked.

Tomlin grunted, walked away from the table, stood beside the bed for a moment, picked up the dirty pillow, dropped it, yanked back the bedclothes, then grabbed the mattress and heaved it on its side against the wall. "Nothing there," Johnnie Brewer remarked.

"Look in the closet," Tomlin directed, and handed Johnnie the flashlight. Tomlin went to the dresser at the foot of the bed.

"For what?" Brewer inquired, strolling toward the closet door.

"For anything you can find," Tomlin said snappishly. He pulled open the dresser drawers, one after another. Dirty under-wear, dirty socks, an old cap, a handful of colored sea shells, a whisk broom worn to a stub, a pair of ragged shuffle slippers, two clean shirts, unironed, a bunch of keys tied together with a bit of cord. Tomlin picked up the keys and held them in his palm thoughtfully. Then Johnnie Brewer struck pay dirt.

"Hey, look at this," he called from inside the closet. Tomlin joined him with a quick, long stride. "On the shelf here," Johnnie said, "back of this stack of magazines."

Tomlin took it out of Johnnie's hand. It was a paper-covered book, grimy, ragged-edged, dog-eared, much studied. Its title was "How to Be a Detective: A Complete Course."

"Well, son of a gun! What do you know about that!" said Johnnie. "How to be a detective!" He laughed suddenly. "A half-wit learning how to be a detective."

"Maybe that's a good start, being a halfwit," Tomlin growled, riffling the pages. A folded paper fell out and Johnnie picked it up and handed it to Tomlin. Tomlin unfolded it and walked back to the light to examine it. it had been crumpled and smoothed out carefully. One corner was missing.

"I'll eat my hat," said Johnnie, "if that ain't the rest of the paper they found in Tuttle's hand, Chief."

The chief said nothing. He was studying the paper. It was a sheet of notepaper and it bore the words:

Walt Darling—
I don't care what happened here in Chicago. I don't think you meant it. I didn't mean what I said to you. I was half crazy when I took that gun and tried to shoot you. Walt darling, won't you forgive me and take me back? I'm sending this airmail and it will be waiting for you in Hamsted and I'm coming to talk with you too. Please think it over, dear. I'll never be a heel again—if you'll give me another chance.
                                                                Sandra

Tomlin read the note twice, then turned it over. A penciled scrawl stared up at him, a scrawl that came downhill on the paper, a scrawl written with terrific effort, the effort of a dying man who had managed one word at a time with the last dribbles of his fast-ebbing life. There were four words.

Leonard Foss shot me.

The chief's brow was frozen in a scowl. "Now who the hell is Leonard Foss?" he muttered.

V

Mike began to bark before the doorbell rang. Ed, jolted out of a sound sleep, sat up in bed and began to swear like a deep-sea sailor. Binnie, who enjoyed the rhythm, was nevertheless forced to put a stop to it. "For Pete's sake, darling," she yawned, "the doorbell's ringing like nuts. Will you go open it or shall I?"

"I'll open it," Ed growled, poking around for his slippers. "Jumping three green eagles, why don't they let a man and his wife sleep! We came to this town for peace and quiet! We haven't got peace and we haven't got quiet! All we've got is grief and headaches and doorbells and, goddam you, take your finger off the bell, I'm coming!"

He went downstairs, dragging his bathrobe after him and trying to get into it. Mike was savage at the front door until Ed slapped his nose and told him to shut up. Ed opened the door. The chief and Johnnie Brewer stood there. The chief looked weary with fatigue. Johnnie was as good as new. "What do *you* want?" Ed asked sourly.

"Want to talk to you."

Ed stared at him sullenly. "The middle of the night," he sneered, "and he wants to talk to me. Go home. I'll talk to you tomorrow."

He tried to close the door but the chief pushed it open and walked in. Mike watched him warily, growling. Ed stepped back in resignation. He shook his head slowly. "Why I don't tell the dog to connect with the seat of your britches," he said, "is more than I know." To Brewer, who waited a little hesitantly outside: "Come on in. Might as well make a party out of it." And then he hollered upstairs to Binnie: "Hey, Bin, Scotland Yard's here again. Come on down while I get pinched some more."

Binnie let out a yelp and came flying along the upper corridor and down the stairs. The chief faced Ed. "Cut the comedy," he said. "Nobody's going to pinch you—yet. All we want you to do is answer some questions. Here. Read this." He handed Ed the note from Sandra Lattimer. Ed read it with an increasing scowl. Binnie, at his side, read it too. Ed finished reading it, turned it over automatically and his frown sharpened suddenly. He looked at Binnie and their eyes met.

"All right," said Tomlin. "Is that Walter Tuttle's handwriting?"

Ed studied the scrawl again. "Yes," he said, "I think so."

"Okay, then who's Leonard Foss?"

Ed scratched his head and his eyes met Binnie's again. "This doesn't make sense," he said.

"What doesn't? You tell me who Leonard Foss is and I'll decide if it makes sense."

Ed bridled. "Okay, I'll tell you. When Walt Tuttle wrote that—"

"Wait a minute!" Johnnie Brewer cut in. "I got it! Look, Chief. These guys, this fellow and Tuttle, they used to write a radio show named *Home Town*. I remember now. Leonard Foss is the name of one of the characters in the show."

The chief scowled at Johnnie and then at Ed. "Is that right?" he asked.

"Mostly," Ed said. "Only the character's name wasn't Leonard Foss; it was Foss Leonard. And what good does that do you?"

That stopped the chief dead in his tracks, but he knew his next move. "Suppose you tell me," he said to Ed. "How do you figure it?"

"How do I figure it? I figure it like this. Walt was shot. He was dying, he was confused. Maybe he tried to write the name of the one who killed him. I think he had the intention of doing just that. But before he could do it, the confusion was greater than his intention. He just wrote a name; he didn't even know what he was writing. The name happened to be the name of a radio character in our show."

"Reversed," the chief pointed out.

"Reversed," Ed nodded.

"Why reversed?"

Ed shrugged. "Your guess is as good as mine."

Johnnie Brewer cut in. "I think I've got it, Chief. Look. Tuttle's been in the habit of thinking of this character by his last name—Leonard. Like, if it was my name, he'd write Brewer first, like in the telephone book. What's more, he's dying, he doesn't know if he'll get it all written, so he writes the important name first—Leonard Then he writes the first name; then he can manage to write: 'shot me.' That makes sense, don't it?"

The chief's smile was scornful. "Does it?" he retorted. "And what does it prove, backwards *or* forwards? It proves he was killed by a character in a radio show. That's a hot one! *I'll* tell you what the whole thing proves: It proves he was out of his head, that's all. He was shot and he was dying and he might have written Santy Claus killed him, for all he knew. He *meant* to write something that made sense, yes; but he couldn't make the grade. He was wandering; he was just about gone; his hand did the writing, not his brain, so he wrote the name of a radio character. That's how important *this* thing is. Isn't that what it looks like to you, MacIntyre?"

Ed passed a slow hand over a fretted brow. "I guess so," he said. He handed back the paper. "Now, if that's all there is to it, is it all right if we go back to bed and get some sleep?"

12
RADIO SCRIPT

I

Ed slept poorly the rest of the night. His mind was at work on the problem like a blacksmith at his anvil. He was awake at six-thirty with a throbbing head. Binnie got up and made breakfast, chiefly of hot coffee.

"I wonder if it's too early to talk to Hastings," Ed mused, looking through eyes squeezed narrow by the ache in his head. "I'd like to know what he thinks."

"Drink another cup of coffee, take a headache powder and call him up and find out."

Ed obeyed and reached Hastings at his home. "I've got an angle," Ed announced. "I'd like to talk it over. I want an opinion."

"Come ahead," Hastings said. "We're just going to have breakfast. Come along and join us."

"I'll have a cup of coffee," Ed told him. "I'll come right along. Where do you live?"

"South Argyle. The other end of Main Street. Number twenty-eight."

"I've seen the street," Ed said. "I'll be there in a few minutes."

Ed put on his hat and coat, kissed Binnie on the end of her nose and went out the front way. He decided not to drive, hoping the walk would clear his head.

It was a big house with a two-car garage accommodating a sedan and a roadster. Leora Hastings opened the door at his ring.

147

"Come in, Mr. MacIntyre. Paul's telephoning. You'll have some breakfast with us?" She was big and blonde and good-looking. The house was furnished in good taste.

"Thanks, I'll just have a little coffee."

She led the way into a breakfast room just as Hastings came to join them. "Glad to see you, Ed. What's on your mind? Sit down. He wants coffee, Leora. You look as if you hadn't slept much, Ed."

"Not much and not well," Ed told him.

"What's on your mind?"

Leora passed him a cup of coffee and he told what had happened the night before. "What do you make out of it, Paul?"

Hastings considered briefly. "I don't know. It needs thought. What do you?"

"You could knock me over with a feather," Ed said wearily. He rubbed his face slowly, as if to push away the fatigue. "I don't agree with Tomlin at all. I think that Walt knew what he was writing when he wrote that. I think he knew he had only a few seconds to live. He started to write what he had to say in the briefest possible way. He started to write 'Leonard shot me.' He must have written just 'Leonard' with a tremendous effort. By the looks of the scrawl, he paused after writing that one word, that one name. Then he must have realized that there must be no confusion about who Leonard was, so he wrote the radio character's first name—Foss. That was a frightful effort too, and the scrawl almost died off after the name Foss, but he managed to add 'shot me,' and that was the end."

"Give me the rest of it," Hastings said. "I don't listen to the radio often. Where do we go from here?"

Briefly Ed sketched the synopsis of the radio serial. "And here, after all these months, I've been writing a radio script about a real murder and I didn't have an inkling. It's plain as day the story's about Calla Forsythe's murder, just the way Walt must have figured it out."

"I don't get it," Hastings frowned. "You mean he knew who killed her and did nothing but write a radio script about it?"

"No." Ed shook his head. "It's more than that, or less than that—I don't know which. After thinking about it most of the night, I've come to the conclusion that Walt suspected who had done it but he didn't have proof. Somehow he figured that putting it into a radio script would do something to the guilty man: drive him into the open, make him show his hand, make him do something to give himself away."

"In other words, he *did* drive him into the open, and got killed for it."

"Yes."

"And according to the script, the killer was a lawyer."

"A lawyer," Ed amended, "who had formerly been a newspaper man. That's one of the reasons I came to you—because you'd know about newspaper men."

Hastings worried over that briefly, then pointed out: "There are only two lawyers in town, Ed."

"Reynolds and Hilliard Wells?"

"That's right."

"Was either of them ever a newspaper man?"

"If he was, he's never let on."

"You'd think he would—to you, wouldn't you? You know them both, don't you; you're on friendly terms with them."

"Certainly," put in Leora Hastings. "They've both been here to dinner."

"Maybe," Hastings mused, "there's a reason why they wouldn't let on."

"Such as what?"

Hastings shrugged. "Who knows? Newspaper men get into trouble sometimes and leave the business and never refer to it again and see that no one else does, either. They go far from the scene of their sins."

"Are Reynolds and Wells from out of town?"

Hastings nodded. "Both of them. Reynolds has been here about twenty years, Hilliard Wells about fifteen."

"Where were they before that?"

"I don't know. I don't recall that I ever did know."

"Would you, as a newspaper man, have any way of finding out about old newspaper men?"

"As much chance as finding what haystack a needle was once in."

Ed finished his coffee. "Well, then, there's another way of finding out: put a private detective agency on both of them. I want this information and I'm going to get it. I'm going to have those two lawyers dug up by the roots."

II

One of the day men pushed Dodo Brown into the chief's office, and the chief got up from his desk with a bitter smile on his face.

"Here he is, Chief. I caught him ducking down Fortner's Alley. He tried to run away. The bump on the front of his head is where he hit the ground when I tripped him up."

The chief nodded, not taking his eyes off Dodo. Dodo nursed the bump on his head and looked balefully back at him.

"Sit down over there," said the chief, but Dodo continued to stand where the last push had left him. "*Sit down over there, I said!*" He spun Dodo around, gave him a shove that sent the boy stumbling double time across the office. The chief followed, snapped him about, and pushed him into the chair so that he sat down with a heavy thud, his head jerking back sharply and remaining that way, the eyes staring with the same dull glare.

"Now look, Brown," the chief said, "I don't want to hurt you, I don't want to get rough with you, but I've stood just about enough nonsense from you. It's about time you did some talking. This is the right time now, and, you're going to talk or I'll know the reason why, you hear me? I want to know everything you know about all this business: all about Tuttle's death and all about Jake Burdick's death and all about that dead baby and everything else you know. Now start talking and start quick if you know what's good for you."

He had thrust his face to within a few inches of the boy's. Dodo turned his face away. "You robbed my room," he mumbled. "You went and robbed my room."

"Robbed your room, did we? We robbed it all right. We robbed it of evidence that you concealed, which is a crime, sonny boy, and if you don't start talking about everything you know, you're going to get slapped in a cell and you're going to stay there until you do talk!"

Dodo's eyes met the chief's now with a calculating little gleam. "Go ahead," he said, "lock me in a cell. Then you got to feed me and I don't have to pay." The humor of it struck him forcefully and he laughed with glee.

The chief turned away in disgust and paced the floor. "If I ever get to be an idiot," he said savagely, "I hope I'm as smart an idiot as this one. Shut up!" he roared, and the boy stopped laughing. The chief paced another hundred yards, then changed face and voice and went in for cajoling and wheedling. "Dodo, look; come on, be a good feller. Where did you get this piece of paper we found in your room? We'll let you go if you tell us. Come on, where'd you get it?"

"You'll let me go?"

"Yes."

The boy hesitated, licked thick lips, eyed the chief thoughtfully for a few seconds, then answered: "I got it out of Mr. Tuttle's hand when he was lying there dead." He fished in a pocket and brought out a pencil stub. "I took this off the table there, too."

Tomlin took the pencil, examined it, laid it on his desk. "When was this?"

"It was when I was in there like I told you I was."

"I see. Tell me about it. Just how did you get the paper and the pencil?"

"Well—he was lying there on the table and he was holding onto the piece of paper tight by the corner, and I tore off the big part, what you got there."

"Why'd you do that? Didn't you know it was evidence the police had to have?"

The boy dropped his eyes and made no reply.

"Did you do it," the chief pressed him, "because you were being a detective?"

The boy mumbled.

"Speak up! You're learning to be a detective, aren't you?"

Dodo nodded.

"And that's why you took the paper, because you thought it was a clue?"

Dodo nodded again.

"Or was there some other reason—were you covering up for somebody—were you hiding that note to protect somebody?"

The boy shook his head.

"Okay, now suppose you tell me why you ran away last night after you brought in the dead baby. Suppose you tell me that?"

The boy looked up with the most innocent of expressions. "I didn't run away," he declared. "I only came with Mr. MacIntyre and brought the—the thing—and then I went away. Nobody told me to stay."

That stopped Tomlin, but he had one more tack.

"Okay, but if you didn't run away, why weren't you in your room when we got there last night?"

"Because I went for a walk," said the boy guilelessly.

"In the middle of the night you went for a walk?" Tomlin queried, his eyes narrowing.

"Yeah."

"Where'd you go?"

"No place. Just for a walk."

"Did you do anything or go to meet anybody?"

"No."

Tomlin threw up his hands. "All right, get out." The boy got up eagerly. "But don't you go anywhere where I can't get hold of you when I want you." The boy promised with an eager head-shake. "Because if you do, we'll get you just the same, and when we do, we won't be as easy on you as we were this time. Understand?"

The big head wagged. The officer at the door opened it and Dodo went scurrying out. Tomlin gazed after him thoughtfully, pulled slowly at his lower lip and said softly: "I wonder—I just wonder."

III

That night the Forsythes broke jail. To this day, no one seems to have the straight story on how it was done. Tomlin swears they were left with no implements whatsoever and must have done it with their teeth. The better suggestion was that Gregg, who had served an apprenticeship with a locksmith, had made an implement out of the buckles from their trouser belts, which had carelessly been left with them. But whatever the method, it worked. The Forsythes were out. Mrs. Forsythe, at the farm, denied any knowledge of their whereabouts. A watch was placed at the farm, but the Forsythe men never returned there.

IV

Ed and Binnie went to Reynolds' office for a cool visit and the reading of Walt's will. When it was over and they were downstairs in the car again, Binnie wept over Walt once more. Nor was it easy for Ed to hold back his tears.

V

It took just one more day for light to dawn on another matter. The light came to Binnie. She pointed it out to Ed: There was another connection between the radio script and the Hamsted real life drama. The name of the murdered girl in the script was Lily. The name of the murdered girl in Hamsted was Calla.

"Calla's a lily," Binnie said. "Walt certainly called that spade a spade."

"A spade that dug his grave," Ed agreed morbidly.

13
EXIT CARL BENJAMIN

I

The telephone in the hall was ringing.

Ed wakened with a start, and Binnie said sharply: "What's that?"

"The telephone," Ed grumbled, and got up and went out into the hall to answer it. His wrist watch said quarter past one in the morning.

It was Hastings. Paul said quietly: "Ed, sorry to get you up, but there's something screwy going on over at your store."

"What do you mean?"

"You'd better not waste any time. I'm calling from the diner. I'd like to go back and keep an eye peeled. How soon can you make it?"

"Five minutes." Ed hung up and went back into the bedroom.

"Five minutes for what?" Binnie was asking sleepily.

"Paul Hastings wants to see me about something," Ed said noncommittally, yawning.

"Does it have to be tonight?"

Ed was dressing. "I don't know. But I might as well go."

"Don't be too long," Binnie murmured, almost asleep. And then she came to with a little start and sat up in the bed. "Are you sure he just wants to see you about something? You aren't getting into something, are you?"

Ed yawned again. "Nope. Be a good girl and go to sleep."

"You wouldn't fib to me, would you, mister?"

"Of course not. Go to sleep."

Hastings was waiting for him in front of the store, which was dark. He motioned for quiet as Ed got out, and together they walked back to the small side street that led off Main, halting at the mouth of the alley that ran behind the block of stores, paralleling Main. There was a stairway down into the alley. At the head of it they halted. There was enough moonlight for them to see the car parked beside the rear door of one of the stores.

"In case you don't know it," Hastings said, "that's the back door of your drug store."

"What's happening?"

"Just wait."

No waiting was necessary. The back door opened and a shadow, only slightly darker than the night before, came out. "Lugging a box," Ed whispered. "Loaded."

The box was placed in the car; the dark figure fumbled at the back door of the store, then turned and got into the car.

"Let's go!" Ed said. He walked quickly down the alley steps. The alley was open at the other end, and the car would have to turn around to drive out.

The lights of the car were turned on, but only the parking lights. The starter hummed, the motor turned over, and then Ed ran for it.

The driver saw him coming. The lights went out. The motor raced madly, gears sang like a buzz saw on steel. The car shot back, swung in an arc, came to a halt with brakes jammed hard, then shot forward with a screaming roar of a motor pressed into frenzied action. The car went straight for Ed and Ed thought of a car coming at him on a dark rainy road, not blacked out like this but with lights blazing. Hastings shouted: "Look out!"

The car missed Ed as he dodged, and Hastings leaped for the running board on the driver's side. He had the door open and was struggling with the driver. He wrenched the wheel over and the car smashed into the brick rear of the store. Ed ran for the car door on the other side, flung it open and grabbed at the man behind the wheel.

Hastings slammed a short punch at a cowering face. The man wilted and Ed yanked him out of the car and propped him up against the brick wall. Hastings came around and struck a match.

It was Carl Benjamin.

"Well, look at what we've got!" said Ed. Benjamin's dark eyes ogled foolishly. He wore no hat and the light of the match shone on his glossy hair, now rumpled from the mauling.

"I'll hold him," Hastings said. "See what he's got in the car." He grabbed Benjamin by the front of his coat and straight-armed him to the wall.

Ed fumbled for the light in the car, turned it on, and opened the rear door. There were three boxes. One contained several cartons of cigarettes and three boxes of expensive cigars; another contained bottles, and packages of patent medicines, a big haul of these; the third contained a connoisseur's selection of expensive perfumes and toilet waters.

"That's a neat haul," Ed said, getting out of the car. He fumbled in his pocket for his keys to the store, opened the door, reached in for a light switch and found it.

"Bring him in, Paul," he said. Hastings shoved Benjamin inside, into the store office. Ed lugged in the boxes of stolen merchandise. Hastings swung a chair around beside the roll-top desk, pushed Benjamin into it and dusted his hands distastefully.

"So it's the sleek little rat!" he said. "I'm not surprised. Ed, I was coming up from the diner and I was just passing the alley when he drove in with his lights dim. That smelled peculiar, so I stopped for a look. When he opened this back door and came in, I called you."

"Thanks, Paul." Ed seated himself in the swivel chair in front of the desk. "All right, what do you say?"

The dark eyes stared balefully.

"I'll take your keys to the store." Ed put out his hand. Reluctantly, silently, Benjamin handed over a key ring. "I'll take your reserve keys too, thanks," said Ed. Benjamin made no move. "Better shell out," Ed advised. "You might get that pretty suit torn if we have to go fishing for them."

Glumly Benjamin pulled out a leather key case, detached several keys and handed them over.

"Thanks," said Ed. "I thought you'd have extras. All shrewd men do. Now suppose you start talking about this sideline of yours." He motioned to the stolen goods on the floor. But Benjamin's mouth was clamped shut and stayed that way.

"Let me try him," Hastings said. "Benjamin, a little light begins to dawn. I wouldn't have given it a thought but for this business tonight. Tell me, how long have you been stealing from this store?"

Benjamin's long slender hand came up and caressed the side of his jaw where Hastings had struck him.

"If you know what's good for you," Hastings went on quietly, "you'll talk. How long have you been stealing?"

The voice came out thin and cracking at first, before it cleared and settled into resignation. "Aw, what difference does it make? You caught me. Go ahead, give me the works. What difference does it make if it's once or ten times or a hundred? You'll give me the works anyhow. So go ahead and give it to me."

"Give you the works, eh?" Hastings repeated slowly. "I wonder, now, if that isn't just what's coming to you." He glanced significantly at Ed, then back at Benjamin. "Benjamin," he said, "I'm going to ask you a question to which I know the answer, so be prepared to answer it without lying. I've spent a lot of time rooting for facts about a lot of people in the last two years—specifically since the Forsythe girl was murdered. To be frank with you, up to the present moment I hadn't picked up anything that seemed especially significant. I picked up a few facts about you that seemed negligible till now; now they're not negligible by any means. Interpreted as the actions of a harmless drug clerk, they seemed as harmless as a drug clerk; as the actions of a thief they look like something else again."

There was a bewildered, frightened look on Carl Benjamin's face.

"Benjamin, when was the last time you saw Calla Forsythe alive?"

The blood drained from Benjamin's face in a split second. "What do you mean? What're you gettin' at?"

"Answer the question. When was the last time you saw the girl?"

"Me? I hardly knew the girl! How do I know when the last time was?"

"She was a customer in the store here, wasn't she?"

"So what—what if she was? We had a lot of customers—"

"Sure you had a lot of customers—and not a pretty girl came in here but you made it a point of getting acquainted."

"What are you gettin' at. You can't—"

"Maybe I can," Hastings cut in. "I'll tell you specifically what I'm getting at. First, answer this question: You were stealing here tonight because you needed money—that's it, isn't it?"

"What does anybody steal for?" Benjamin replied savagely. "Sure I need money! What do they pay me here—enough so you can get it under your thumb nail! Sure I need money. I'm in deep. I need plenty and—"

"Gambling? That's it, isn't it?"

"What the hell difference does it make what it is? Go ahead, pinch me; go on, call the cops!"

"Not just yet. I said I'd tell you what I'm getting at, and I'm going to. A man who will steal in order to pay his debts is rotten stuff, just the type who would do to Calla Forsythe what was done to her."

Benjamin sat back slowly in the chair, his eyes fixed on Paul Hastings. "Take it easy now," he said slowly. "Take it easy. Don't you go saying I killed that girl."

"Do you still say that you barely knew her?"

"Sure I still say it."

"You're a liar, Benjamin, and you make the molehill of evidence look like a mountain. I have positive proof that you took Calla Forsythe driving in your car a few days before her death, that you drove north out of town and parked and that she got out of your car and walked home."

"That's a dirty lie!"

Hastings was nodding slowly. "Of course. Everything about you is a dirty lie. Unfortunately for you, I have the facts from a very reputable person whose word against yours in front of a murder jury—"

Benjamin jumped up out of his chair. A thin hand clawed
pleadingly at Paul Hastings' coat. "For God's sake, mister, don't
talk like that! Don't go pinning anything like that on me. I'll tell
you what happened, but it wasn't any murder!"

"Sit down."

Benjamin sank into his chair and passed a shaking hand
through his black hair.

"Look, Mr. Hastings. This is the straight lowdown. I was out
after Calla Forsythe—yes. I thought she was easy stuff and I—"

"What made you think that?"

"I don't know. I just thought so. So I asked her if she'd go for
a little ride in the car. That was the only time I ever took her out."

"What happened?"

Benjamin twisted his fingers nervously. "Nothing. I got her
out on the road and when I tried to neck with her she got out of
the car and walked home."

"When was that?"

"A few days before she died. I don't remember how many days
exactly."

"You didn't try again after that?"

"No"

"Are you sure?"

"Sure I'm sure."

"Had you been out with her before that?"

"No."

"And that's all you ever had to do with her?"

Hastings looked at Ed. "Okay, Ed, he's all yours. Call the
station and have them pick him up on this larceny."

But Carl came out of his chair like a spring released, and before Ed or Hastings could lay a hand on him he had flung open
the door and bolted into the darkness. Ed and Paul Hastings ran
a few steps after him; then they gave it up, for it was only too
plain that Benjamin had more than an edge in a footrace.

They went back into the store. "Call the cops," Hastings said.

"To hell with it," Ed declared wearily. "I'll tell 'em tomorrow.
Tell 'em tonight and they'll have me up the rest of another night.
I'm groggy, and I'd rather not see Tomlin's face right now."

Ed went home and got into bed.

"Did you have a nice chat?" Binnie asked out of a maze of sleep.

"Dandy," said Ed. "I'll tell you about it in the morning."

In the morning he reported the theft to Tomlin, who bawled him out for the delay.

The delay was a sufficient one. Carl Benjamin had vanished completely.

14

MAN WITH A PAST

I

Monahan, the private detective Ed had engaged through the Boston branch of a national agency, took out a leather pocket secretary and unfolded several sheets of paper.

"We have absolutely nothing," he said, "on Absalom Reynolds. We traced him back to law school but no further. He came out of no place and left no trace behind him." He referred to a second sheet. "The other one is a pip. Hilliard Wells, the fat one. Our Toledo office dug up quite a bit on him. His real name is Harry Wellman. He has a wife and two children, all living. He was a newspaper man in Toledo. A little more than eighteen years ago he ducked out on his wife and children—with another woman. One of the children was two years old, the other six months. The other woman got lost on the way; there's no trace of her. Wells, or Wellman, turned up on the West Coast. He got himself a law degree in a little jerk law school in Los Angeles. Our Los Angeles office says he was a complete flop in legal practice. He folded up out there and disappeared. There's no trace of him after that, except here in Hamsted. He's been here about fifteen years, so it looks as if he came directly here. He seems to have done okay for himself. He's one of the two lawyers in town. He lives well, steps out on the sly with another man's wife, and seems to enjoy it."

"The crummy rat," said Binnie quietly.

Monahan looked up from his notes. "This was a quick job," he said. "I've got affidavits here from Toledo and I'll get others from the West Coast as soon as possible, maybe in a day or two. There may even be something in later today."

Ed thought about it for several seconds. "Well, now that we've got it, what do we do with it?"

"Well, I'll tell you," said Monahan. "What we have doesn't prove anything, but it might serve to scare him into admitting something."

"You mean lay it on a platter and see what he does?"

"Yes."

"With the police?"

"It isn't ripe for the police yet. But I'd have a competent witness handy."

"Paul Hastings," Binnie suggested. "He owns and edits the local paper," she explained to Monahan.

"Fair enough," Monahan agreed. "When do we start?"

"The sooner the better," said Ed.

II

It was not until five o'clock that they found Hilliard Wells in his office.

"Who's going to handle this?" Hastings asked as they passed through the waiting room.

"Suits me if you do," said Ed.

"Okay," Hastings nodded, and his eyes were grim and bright, "then let's rush him and catch him off balance. It may help. Let's go."

He went to the door marked: "Mr. Wells. Private," threw it open and walked in. Ed and Monahan followed. Monahan closed the door.

Hilliard Wells, sitting at his desk, looked up with a startled, annoyed expression. The little eyes in his chubby, pink face looked at all three of his visitors, one at a time. They lingered momentarily on Ed, frowned briefly at Monahan and came to rest on Hastings.

"What do you want, gentlemen?" he said quietly.

Hastings pulled up a chair and sat down. Ed and Monahan remained standing.

"I hear you don't like the newspaper business, Mr. Wells," said Hastings casually.

Wells stared. "What are you talking about?" he demanded. "I've got nothing against you, Hastings."

"Against me? I didn't say that. I hear you were a newspaper man once upon a time and gave it up. That's right, isn't it?"

A fine cobweb of a frown puckered the lawyer's brow. "What is this, a joke?" he asked. "Look, Hastings, I'm not in the mood for this. Suppose you peddle the gag somewhere else." He leaned forward belligerently, both of his little fat hands flat on the desk before him, his little eyes sharp with anger.

"It's no gag," Hastings said. "This is the real McCoy. Mr. Wells, when was the last time you saw Calla Forsythe?"

"Now, just a minute!" Wells got to his feet, pushing back his chair. "I told you I was in no mood for a gag. And I'm not in a mood for answering questions that don't concern me. Now, get out of here, all of you." A fat index finger pointed the way.

Hastings' face was grim as he leaned forward in his chair. "Just a minute, Mr. Wellman. Maybe you won't have to answer questions. Maybe we can answer them for you. First of all I'll start answering all the questions about your identity. In the first place, your true name is Harry Wellman—"

"Get out of here!" said Hilliard Wells.

"In the second place, you have a wife and two children alive in Toledo."

"Get out of here before I call the police!"

"You deserted them for another woman. You changed your name. You left the newspaper business and became a lawyer. You came here to our town and for fifteen years you've been playing around with other men's wives—"

"You dirty—" Words failed Wells. He grabbed up the telephone. "Give me the police station!"

"But other men's wives weren't enough for you. You went after a little girl named Calla Forsythe. You got her in trouble and then—"

"Hello. Police station. Is Tomlin there? Let me speak to him. This is Hilliard Wells. All right—tell him there are three hoodlums in my office and I want him to send someone down right away and throw them out!"

Hastings turned his head and winked at Ed and Monahan. He got up. "All right, Wellman," he said. "We'll get out. We need a few more affidavits to tie this thing up tight. Those affidavits are on their way here right now. When they get here, we'll be the ones to call Tomlin, not you."

He led the way out of the office, Ed and Monahan following, and as they went they heard Wells calling off Tomlin's dogs. Downstairs, Monahan said: "I'm going to call the office. Maybe something else has come in."

"Then let's get back to the house," Ed suggested.

"Wait a minute!" Hastings had an idea. "I've got a hunch on how to work this out with that heel. Monahan, have you got the address of his wife in Toledo?"

"Sure." He fumbled in his pocket for a notebook, fingered through the pages and showed the address to Hastings. Hastings jotted it down.

"What are you going to do?" Ed asked.

"I'm going to try a little melodrama; maybe it'll work."

Ed looked at Monahan, who shrugged. "Just don't take any fancy chances," Monahan advised. "I'd rather do it with facts instead of melodrama. And maybe the facts are waiting for us now."

"Watch your step," said Ed.

"I will," Hastings assured him. "And I'll phone you as soon as I get something."

III

Hastings waited in the lobby of the building for about fifteen minutes. A few stragglers drifted out. Hilliard Wells was still in his office.

Dusk was coming down like a gray blanket when Hastings started up the stairs. The building was silent except for his footsteps and the sound of a big clock somewhere in the building, ticking a rhythmic accompaniment to the footsteps. At the top

of the stairs, Hastings turned to the right down the dim unlight-
ed corridor towards Hilliard Wells' office.

No light was burning in Wells' outer office. Hastings went in
quietly, closed the door softly. A shaft of lemon-yellow light fell
through the frosted glass of the inner office door. Hastings could
hear Wells moving about. He heard the opening and closing of
drawers and the sound of footsteps, and once a muttered word or
two, unintelligible through the door.

Hastings laid a hand on the knob, twisted it quickly, opened
the door and stepped in. The lawyer was standing in front of
a large, old-fashioned safe whose door was swung wide open.
He was rooting in a mass of papers on the floor of the safe. He
straightened up quickly as Hastings came in, turned, and was
still as a frozen image for several seconds.

"Busy?" Hastings asked. He closed the door behind him and
stood with his back to it. There was a small hard smile on his
face. "Going somewhere?"

Wells dusted his hands carefully, then came forward and sat
down at his desk.

"What do you want, Hastings?"

Hastings moved toward the desk at a leisurely pace, pulled
up a chair and sat down. "I asked if you were going somewhere?"

The little eyes in the plump face were like bright black beads.
"Why should I go any place?"

"You ought to know. Unless I miss my guess, what you've just
been doing is sorting out what you want to take. You think you're
running away, don't you, Mr. Wells, or Wellman, or whatever
your name is?"

"You're crazy." The fat little hands folded themselves on the
desk, the fingers gripped hard, and the buffed nails gleamed in
the light. "I told you before, and I'm telling you again, I don't
want to hear any more poppycock about anyone named Wellman, and I don't want you to call me Wellman. I don't know
what you're talking about or what you're getting at—"

"Oh, you don't? Then suppose we get down to fundamen-
tals." He reached out and drew the telephone closer to him. He

lifted the receiver and asked for the toll operator. Wells' eyes never left Hastings' face; he remained absolutely still except for the slow blinking of his eyelids. "Hello. Toll operator? Operator, this is 1357. I want to get Toledo, Ohio, Mrs. Harry Wellman, 2860 Blanca Drive. I want to speak personally with—"

Quick as a striking snake, Wells shot out a hand that cut off the telephone connection. He snatched the cradle of the phone sharply toward him. Hastings jumped to his feet, started to go around the desk. He dropped the receiver and Wells put it in its place.

"So you admit you're Wellman, you dirty little rat!" Hastings said. "Well, you won't get away with it!"

But Wells was going to get away with it for the time being. He was on his feet backing away from Hastings; he yanked open a desk drawer, snatched out a black, short-muzzled gun and fired a single shot.

Hastings stopped the bullet and the bullet stopped him. His eyes went wide and his mouth fell open in a helpless way. He rocked unsteadily, then plunged forward suddenly, fell across Wells' swivel chair and slid heavily to the floor.

There was a complete silence except for the ticking of the clock on Wells' desk. Wells kept moving slowly, automatically, noiselessly backward on the carpeted floor, the gun still pointed at the spot where Hastings had been. There was sweat on his forehead and in his palms; his lips were gray.

The phone rang. Wells halted abruptly in his backward march. The phone rang again. Wells seemed not to know what the sound was. It rang a third time. Wells shook his head in a little jerky movement, as if a spasm had shot through him. He looked quickly at the office door, then strode to the desk, put down the gun, picked up the receiver, and said in a croaking voice: "Hello."

It was the operator. She wanted to know if the party who had asked for the Toledo call still wished to have it put through.

Wells cleared his throat.

"No," he said. "It isn't necessary. Cancel the call, please."

He hung up, picked up the gun and pocketed it, and went quickly to the door. He turned the key in the lock, tried the knob to make sure no one could get in. Then he went back to the phone, called a number, and waited stonily while the phone rang several times. A woman answered at last. "Hello."

"Hello." Wells cleared the croak out of his voice and spoke sharply. "Hello, Anna. Anna, listen to me. Pack a bag. I've got to get out of town. You're going with me."

"What are you talking about, Hill?" the woman asked. "What do you mean, you've got to get out of town?"

"There's no time to argue!" Wells snapped. "I'll meet you in an hour, you know where."

"But—what about my husband?" the woman asked in quick anguish.

"Your husband be damned! You're either coming with me or you aren't! Now which is it?"

He heard an indrawn breath. There was a brief silence. Then: "All right, Hill," she said in a strained, empty voice. "I'll meet you."

"One hour," he said, and hung up.

He went to the safe, hastily sorted out a few papers, shoved them into a briefcase, then carried the rest to the fireplace at the opposite end of the office. He put them on the grate and touched a match to them. Red and yellow flame began to devour them. Several times he went back and forth from the safe to the fireplace, then from the green filing case to the fire, then from the bookcase. The flames leaped and danced crazily about papers and books.

Wells turned off the desk light and in the firelight slipped on his overcoat, quickly opened one desk drawer after another, put some of the contents in his pockets, some in the briefcase. Then for a moment or two he stood looking down at the silent, motionless Hastings.

After that he buttoned up his coat, walked briskly to the coat tree to get his hat, unlocked his office door, crossed the outer office and stepped out into the hall.

Without bothering to lock the outer door, he went down the almost dark corridor, down the stairs and out into the street.

15

A FOOL DEPARTS

I

Darkness had come quickly. Monahan had made a fruitless phone call to his office in Boston and had left Hamsted. Ed waited uneasily for Hastings' call, but it didn't come. At last he phoned Hastings' house.

"No, he's not here," Leora Hastings said. "Maybe he's at the office."

But the newspaper office didn't answer.

They had supper. "I wonder if anything's happened to him," Ed worried.

"He's big enough to take care of himself," Binnie said. "He'll call you when he's ready."

"I know, but just the same—"

Mike began to bark savagely. He lunged at the front door and ran back and forth from the door to the windows.

"Do we have company?" Binnie queried.

Ed went to the door and opened it. "Shut up, Mike!" he ordered. "For crying out loud, stop bellowing!"

Mike subsided into a growl. The light from the living room lay like a thin carpet across the porch. A brisk fall wind was talking in a whisper in the big trees on the lawn. Ed turned on the porch light and stepped out. "Ed, you'll catch cold," Binnie called out.

Ed came in and closed the door, turned out the porch light. He looked puzzled.

"All right?" Binnie asked.

Ed scratched his neck. "I didn't hear anybody. But I think I *felt* somebody. Or I'm nuts."

Then he opened the door again. Footsteps came solidly up the front walk. Ed snapped on the porch light once more. A man came belligerently up the steps and across the porch.

"MacIntyre, I want to talk to you."

It was Absalom Reynolds. His lean, dark face was taut with anger and he pointed a warning finger at Ed, ignoring Ed's invitation to come inside. "Look, MacIntyre: this is a little warning to you. Either you call off these people that are trying to investigate me or you're going to find yourself in more trouble than you bargained for!"

"Now, just a minute."

"I haven't a minute to spare you!" the lawyer snapped. "It's just one way or the other. Suit yourself!"

He turned and walked across the porch, down the steps and down the path to the street and was gone in the darkness.

Ed closed the door and turned to Binnie with a shrug.

"Tough guy," he said. Then he frowned and turned back to the door. "That's funny. The dog hears someone and barks, I open the door, there's no one there, and then all of a sudden *that* one comes barging up the walk."

Mike began to bark once more.

"Here we go again," said Ed. He opened the door. This time it came at once. Footsteps on the front path, coming at a trot.

Ed peered into the darkness.

Dodo Brown came up the front steps. "Mr. MacIntyre!" he said breathlessly.

"Hello. Come in."

The boy came in and Ed closed the door. "Mr. MacIntyre, someone's after me!"

"Sit down," said Ed. "Get your breath. What do you mean, someone's after you?"

The boy sat on the edge of a big armchair, dropped his hat on the floor between his feet and wrung his hands. "I dunno," he said, and shivered as if he were cold.

Ed sat down opposite him. "Look, Dodo—look, Will," he corrected himself, "pull yourself together. Take it easy. Want a drink of water?"

Binnie already had it there for him. Dodo took the glass and gulped half its contents, nodded his thanks and handed the glass back.

"Now," Ed began again, "who's after you?"

The boy shook his head in a bewildered way. "I dunno," he repeated. "I dunno who it is."

"How do you know anybody's after you?"

"I saw them."

"Where'd you see them?"

"In"—the boy hesitated—"in a dream."

"Oh, come on now, Will. You aren't afraid of anything you saw in a dream."

"Yessir, I am. I dreamed the dream three times. And they say"—he gulped—"they say when you dream it three times it comes true."

Mike began to bark viciously again. He leaped up from his corner and divided his attention between the door and the windows.

"That," said Ed, getting up, "is enough. All right, Mike—into the kitchen with you." He took the protesting dog by the collar and led him into the kitchen. "Now get in there and pipe down."

He closed the door and went back to Dodo Brown. "Okay, Dodo, tell me about it. What did you dream three times?"

The boy put his fingers inside his collar and moved them back and forth in a distressed way. "I dunno as I ought to tell."

"Why not?"

"Because—in the dream—the same one came three times and said I'd get killed if I told."

"If you told what?"

"If I told who it was and what I did."

"But you came to tell me who it was, didn't you, and what you did?"

The boy swallowed hard. "I dunno," he said, looking about him uneasily.

"When did you have these dreams?"

"Two nights ago I had the first one, then last night I had the second one, then just now I had the third one."

"Just now?"

"Yeah."

"You were sleeping just before you came here?"

"Yessir. I went home to my room and I lay down for a nap, like I sometimes do. I went to sleep and I dreamed it." He wrung his hands nervously.

"You dreamed," Ed pressed him, "that someone came and threatened to kill you if you told?"

"Yessir."

"Well, if you don't want to tell, why did you come here to see me? You must have had some reason."

"Sure. I had a reason. I don't hafta tell anything"—he looked about him craftily—"but I can show you somethin'."

"What?"

"I can't tell you, but I'll show you."

"All right, show me. Have you got it here?"

The big head shook. "It's buried."

Ed's stomach turned over. He caught Binnie's eye; she was pale. "Dodo, you mean—another body?"

"No." The big head shook again. "Something else."

"Well, what, Will? *What is it?*"

The boy licked dry lips, and when he spoke it was reluctantly. "It's books," he said. "Burned books."

"What kind of books? Whose books? Who burned them?"

"I ain't tellin' no more. It ain't safe."

"Can you tell me who buried them?"

A nod. "Sure. *I* did. And that's all I can tell."

It seemed best to pamper his warped mind. "Okay. You're going to take me to it. When shall we go?"

"Now," said the boy eagerly. "While it's dark, so's no one won't see."

"Okay. You wait here. I'll get my hat and coat."

The shovels were still in the car. Ed and Dodo went out the front way and around back to the garage. They were backing out, down the driveway to the street, when Mike began his noise again.

"He's got the jitters," Ed said. "Now, which way, Will?"

The boy pointed a crooked finger east down Walden Street. "Down here, then go right."

Ed drove the short block to Proctor Street and turned north. "How far?" he asked.

The boy peered into the solid darkness broken only by the puny light of widely separated street lamps high on telephone poles. "Over Burke's Hill. Where the three trees are."

"Three trees! There'll be a million trees out this way, Will."

"Three trees together," said the boy quietly. "All alone. Three of 'em, all alone—together."

Half a mile and they left the inadequate street lights behind. Broad fields sprawled away to right and left. Dodo was uneasy. He kept looking over his shoulder at the black road behind them.

"What's the matter?" Ed asked.

"I dunno," the boy said. But he was restless.

And then Ed caught the same feeling that something was wrong somewhere; specifically what it was, he could not say.

Suddenly Dodo snapped his head to one side and listened over his shoulder for sounds from behind. After several seconds he turned abruptly in the seat to scan the road again through the rear window. "There's somebody coming!"

Ed took another look in the mirror. "There's nobody coming, Will," he said. "Now, *you* aren't going to get jittery on me, are you?"

"There's somebody coming!" the boy insisted. "I know there's somebody coming!"

Ed ran the car over to the side of the road, brought it to a stop, and turned off the motor. He opened the car door, stuck his head out and listened. After half a minute he closed the door again and shook his head. "There's nobody back there, Will."

The boy was still listening intently. Then he scratched his head and mumbled slowly and thoughtfully: "That's the way I get sometimes. I feel things. Sometimes they're there, sometimes they ain't. I dunno. I get mixed up."

Ed started the car again and held it at thirty-five. "How much farther, Will?"

"Just over the hill."

They topped the dark crest and the boy said suddenly: "In the field over there!" He was pointing away to the right.

Ed jerked the car to a stop. It was too dark to see Dodo's three trees, but he peered in that direction.

"Let's go!" said Dodo. He had forgotten his nervousness in the excitement of what was to come. He threw open the door and ran forward. The outer rays of the headlights caught him as he turned to gesture eagerly for Ed to come on.

That was the last of Dodo Brown. From back there in the darkness a gun cracked the quiet night wide open. As the first shot hit him, Dodo spun around like a mechanical doll, arms flung out, and then crashed face down in roadside brush as another shot stopped his pirouetting as suddenly as the first shot had begun it. It was a short dance of death for Dodo Brown, and Ed crouched back from it, back and down, huddling on the front seat. His hand shot out and extinguished the car lights. He felt bullets hit the car. Then the shooting stopped.

A car roared into action. Ed sprang up. Staring hard into the gloom, he saw its evil bulk swing around in the faintest of moonlight. It was gone in an instant, blending with darkness that was more potent than the moonlight. The car was going back to town.

Ed got out into the road quickly, the flashlight from the steering post rack in his hand. Dodo lay spread-eagled in the bushes. Ed turned him over.

It was quite horrible. Ed picked him up and put him on the back seat of the car.

He drove at top limit, accelerator pedal down to the floor. But he didn't catch up with the other car, which had vanished like black smoke in a blacker pit.

16

DIG AGAIN

I

Binnie was gray-lipped. "Ed, it could have been you! If you had got out of the car first, it *would* have been you!"

"I suppose so." Ed sat in the armchair, leaning forward, elbows on his knees, his face in both hands, fingers nervously massaging his forehead. "Yes, I suppose so."

"What did the chief say?"

Ed rubbed his eyes slowly. "He wasn't there. He's out of town. He's up in Boston, interviewing Sandra Lattimer."

"Sandra Lattimer in Boston!"

"Yeah. She flew here at his request or his order or whatever it was. She took sick on the plane, so he's interviewing her in Boston. Anyway, the cop Brewer took my statement in writing and I signed it. We carried poor Dodo downstairs and stretched him out on a cot in a cell and threw a piece of canvas over him. And that's the end of poor old Dodo. . . . Don't call me Dodo, he said; call me Will. . . . Poor duffer. I wish we knew everything that was going on in that big head of his. For a bird that everybody called the town moron, he seemed to know pretty much what he was doing. I think perhaps he actually did know more than anybody else about the whole thing." He looked up at Binnie. "No word from Paul Hastings?"

"Not a word."

Ed got up, went to the telephone and called the Hastings' home. Leora Hastings answered.

"No," she said, "Paul isn't here. I don't know where he is. He should have been home by now, or he should have called me; he always does."

"He isn't at the office?"

"No. I just phoned. He's not there."

"Ask him to phone me as soon as you hear from him." When he had hung up he went back to his chair and sat down. Mike came over and put his head on Ed's knee. Ed stroked the big head and silken ears in a slow mechanical way.

Suddenly a horrible thought struck him. He got up quickly and went back to the telephone, thumbed through the phone book.

"What now?" Binnie asked. "You look scared."

Ed picked up the receiver and called Hilliard Wells' office. After a brief pause, he heard the operator ringing. There was no answer. Then ringing went on persistently.

He was about to hang up when the receiver at the other end was lifted. "Hello!" said Ed. "Hello!"

Then he heard a moan and a voice that mumbled something incoherent.

"Hastings!" Ed hollered. "Paul Hastings! Is that you? What's the matter? Paul, what's the matter? Can you hear me?" He heard the mumbling again, the moaning sound again very close to the receiver, a gasp and then the sound of the receiver tumbling to the desk. "Paul! Paul! Paul Hastings!" Only a faint moan and heavy breathing now.

Ed hung up and ran to the den for his hat and coat. Binnie was at his heels. "What's the matter, Ed? Where did you call? What's the matter?"

"He's at Wells' office. Something's happened to him. He's hurt."

Binnie grabbed up her own hat and coat that lay handy on the couch. "Okay, let's go." She was in the hall and out the back door before he could frame a protest. He followed her into the garage.

"Binnie, get out of here. You get back in the house." She was already in the car. The starter whirred, the motor turned over.

He got in beside her. "Look, Binnie." She backed the car out like a shot, swung it into the street and headed for the center of town. "All right," said Ed resignedly. "Let's go."

Hastings' car stood in front of the office building. Binnie shot the car to the curb and jammed on the brakes with a jerk that snapped Ed's head like a knot on a whip.

He reached into the car for the flashlight and went into the dark building, Binnie at his side. They went up the stairs and down the corridor to Wells' office. Ed had a restraining hand on Binnie's arm. "*I* go in first," said he.

"Right, my love," said Binnie.

Wells' office door was dark; no light pierced the glass in the frame. Ed grabbed the knob, turned and thrust. It was open. He shot the light in. Nobody there. "Wait here," he whispered to Binnie.

"Sure," said Binnie, and walked in with him.

He glowered sourly at her, then went quickly across the outer office to the door that said: "Mr. Wells." He opened it quickly simultaneously straight-arming Binnie out of the path of anything that might come through the door.

His light found Paul Hastings at the desk. He was sitting in the chair, slouched forward in a pose reminiscent of that last pose of Walt's. One arm was flung out across the desk. The telephone was just out of reach of the curled fingers.

Ed was inside and beside him before Binnie got her balance after Ed's shove. Then she came running in. "Is he—Ed, he isn't—?"

Ed was bending over him. "Paul! . . . He's breathing," he said to Binnie.

Hastings' breath burbled in and out of his mouth. Ed moved him gently back in the chair, so that his arm and band slid off the desk and fell into his lap. "Blood!" gasped Binnie

Hastings seemed to hear her and opened his eyes. He stared at her almost as if he did not see her, then his head fell a little to one side and he looked at Ed. He took a deep breath with difficulty and closed his eyes at the pain. "Get me out of here," he said. "Get me home."

"We'd better get a doctor first," Binnie said.

"Home," Hastings repeated, and opened his eyes again. "Get me out of this damn place." And he grimaced painfully.

Ed got his shoulder under Hastings' arm and helped him to his feet. Binnie came around on the other side to help and together they got him out of the office, down the steps, out of the building and into the back seat of the car. "We ought to take him up to the hospital, Ed," Binnie insisted.

"Damn hospitals!" Hastings groaned. "Ed, please get me home and get Doc Jenkins. I'll be all right."

Binnie drove and Ed supported Hastings in the back seat. They drove down Main Street, into Argyle at Ed's direction, and pulled up in front of Hastings' house.

"Now you can do something," Ed said. "Go in and prepare his wife for what's coming."

Binnie got out of the car, ran up to the door and rang the bell. Ed had started to help Hastings out of the car when Binnie and Leora Hastings came down the path at a run. "Paul, are you all right?"

Hastings grinned feebly. "I'm okay," he said. "It isn't bad. Heavy caliber. Took me in the shoulder. Knocked me out but I'll be okay. Messy, that's all." He stumbled and Ed steadied him, got him up the porch steps and inside.

"Where to?" Ed asked. "Can you make it upstairs to a bedroom?"

"Sure," said Hastings; "let's go."

Leora Hastings ran up ahead of them.

"Binnie, call the doctor," Ed said.

"What doctor?"

"Jenkins," Leora called out. "He's in the book. The phone's in the alcove."

Binnie turned back and went downstairs. Ed got Hastings into his bedroom and helped him onto the bed. He lay back and closed his eyes. His wife opened his coat, vest and shirt and gave a little gasp at the wound. Hastings opened his eyes and grinned sardonically at her white face.

"There must be something I can do before the doctor comes," she said.

"There is," said Hastings. "Get me a good slug of whiskey."

She went out quickly and Hastings was silent for a minute; then he looked at Ed and said: "That little stinker Wells—I made a pass at calling his bluff—"

"What did you do?"

"I started to put in a call for his wife in Toledo. He yanked out a gun and let me have it right across the desk. And that was all, brother."

"Not quite," said Ed. "Dodo Brown got it tonight."

Hastings had closed his eyes. They opened quickly now. "Got it?" he echoed. "What happened?"

"He's dead," Ed went on. "Shot. And it could have been me, Paul. And maybe it will be me—next."

Pain closed Hastings' eyes again. Ed was silent till he opened them once more. "This'll wait till some other time," he said. "You're in no shape for news like this."

Hastings swore petulantly. "Dammit!" he said, "quit treating me like an invalid! I've got a little bullet hole in me and I've lost a little blood! Maybe it won't be you next; maybe it'll be me again. I want to know how things stand. What happened, Ed?"

Ed shrugged, and told him the details.

II

Ed ran the car into the driveway. "Okay, Toots," he said. "This is as far as you go."

Binnie had started to get out. She stopped and turned slowly to face him. "What do you mean, as far as *I* go? Where are *you* going?"

"Never mind. I'll be back in half an hour."

"Ed, I want to know where you're going."

"Me? Why, I'm going—I'm going—uh—I'm going down to report the shooting to the chief of police. You know bullet wounds have to be reported, Binnie," he finished weakly.

"Ed, that's a pretty bum lie! The doctor said he was going to report the bullet wound."

"Look, Binnie, please get out and mind your own business, will you, please?"

"Well, I like that! If this isn't my business, I'd like to know what is."

"Will you get out and stop arguing?"

"No. I will not!"

"Binnie, do I have to get around there and drag you out?"

"That's the only way you'll get me out! I know where you're going, Mister MacIntyre. You're going back to the place where Dodo took you. You're going to try to find those three trees and do a little digging!"

"All right, so I'm going to find the three trees and do a little digging! What's that got to do with you?"

"It's got this to do with me: I'm going too!"

"You are in a duck's ear! Look, Binnie; you heard what I said: Get out of the car before I yank you out on your nose!"

"That's the only way you'll ever get me out, brother. You heard me."

"Okay! If that's the way you feel about it, I'll yank you out!"

He got out of the car and stalked around to the other side. But Binnie was too smart for him. She slammed her door and his, flipped down the lock on both of them, slipped under the wheel and sent the car shooting backward down the drive.

"Hey!" Ed hollered. "Hey! Come back here, you little stinker! Binnie, you cut it out! You come back here!" He went running after her. She swung the car out into the street and shot away toward Proctor Street. Ed ran after her frantically.

"Binnie, for Pete's sake, come back here! Binnie, you come back! You hear me?"

She stopped the car suddenly with a screaming of brakes. Ed came running up alongside. He rattled the handle of the car door beside Binnie. "Binnie, don't be a fool! Open up. Let me in."

"Stop screaming!" she said. "You'll bother the neighbors."

"Binnie, where the devil do you think you're going? Open this door! You hear me?"

"Ed MacIntyre, with you or without you I'm going over to Burke's Hill and find three trees and dig. I don't know what I'm going to find or what I'm going to do with it when I find it. But I'm going to do it, just the same. I'd much rather you'd go along, but whether you go or not, *I'm* going. What's sauce for the goose is what you're getting. Now, which is it? Are you coming or do I go alone?"

"Binnie, you're absolutely, totally nuts!"

"Okay. Then I'm going alone."

"All right. All right. You win. Open the door."

"No tricks now."

"Okay, no tricks."

Thereupon Binnie opened the door beside the driver's seat and slid over. "All right, let's go."

Ed got in, grumbling. "I'll never forgive myself for this," he said. "I'm a sap and a dope and soft-spined fool. And you're a fool too!" He turned hotly to her. "Don't you know there's apt to be some of the same business—bullets?"

"I know," she said calmly. "What's for you is for me, sweetie pie."

"That's very noble, my little dove. Maybe we'll both get it."

"Maybe," said Binnie. "Maybe not. Start driving, Butch."

"Okay," he said, and swung into Proctor Street. They sped quickly out of the lighted portion of the street. The lights of the car cut a canyon in the wall of darkness. It was even darker than on the trip with Dodo. The moon was hidden and the fields that lay on both sides were masked in gloom. There were no other cars visible.

In a few minutes they shot up Burke's Hill, and as they came to the crest Ed slowed, ran the car off the road into a field, stopped and yanked on the brake. Then he turned out the lights quickly.

"This time," he said, "we get out in the dark. And I get out first. Stay where you are." He got out, walked around the front of the car to Binnie's side, stood looking and listening in the dark; then opened Binnie's door.

"Maybe we should have brought Mike," she said.

"Scared now?"

"No!"

"That's good. I'm scared stiff. I'm glad somebody's brave."

"Do I get out now?"

"If you're coming."

She got out and he closed the door.

"Which way do we go?" she asked.

"All I know," said Ed, "is that it's off to the right here."

"The moon'll be out soon," Binnie pointed out. "It's on its way."

"That'll be a help."

"Well, let's get started. You've got the flashlight, haven't you?"

"Sure. Wait till I get a shovel."

"Get one for me too."

"Stop being a girl scout. I'll do the shoveling. You can be the moral support."

"Okay."

Ed got a shovel out of the car and shouldered it like a musket. "Come on."

Following the beam of the big flashlight, they started across the field at a good pace. "If we find this spot," said Ed, "we're pretty good."

"There comes the moon," said Binnie. The curtain of clouds that hid the moon rode along on the wind. Briefly there was a gray glimmer, and then the clouds split away and the moon, nearly full, looked down.

"That's better," said Ed, hiking along. "But I still don't see three trees. Furthermore, the more moonlight, the better target we'll make."

"We're a pretty good target just with the flashlight," she said. "A little moonlight more or less won't matter."

After several moments of silence Ed said thoughtfully: "I figure it this way. The boy would have had me stop on the road as near as possible to the spot where the trees were. That means we keep going on a line straight down from the car. I don't think we have to worry about—"

"Trees dead ahead," said Binnie. They hurried their steps. It was a small grove of pines, perhaps a dozen.

"I don't see three especially together," Ed said. "The whole damn bunch are together." They went through the grove and out into the open again, then halted as Ed sent the light searching

ahead. The long beam caught a towering black form some twenty
yards away, then another of the right, and another beside that.

"Three in a line," said Binnie. "That's it, Ed."

"Let's go."

They were three giants, standing apart from the other trees,
guarding Dodo's last secret.

"I'll make you a bet he talked to all three of 'em," Ed said.

"Never mind the philosophy. Where do we dig?"

"Hold this a minute." He handed her the shovel and went
searching the ground at the foot of the trees. It was a much
simpler job than finding the burial spot in the Forsythe grove.
Behind the center tree was a spot covered more thickly with pine
needles than the surrounding area. Ed kicked the needles away.
Beneath them was freshly turned earth, earth tamped down by
heel and sole.

"This is it, Binnie. Take the light. Give me the shovel."

It was brief digging this time. The boy had hollowed out,
probably with his hands, a hole not much more than a foot and
a half deep and a foot across. In it he had buried a round tin can
with a lid. Ed lifted it out. Binnie dropped to her knees beside
him. "Open it up!" she said with hushed eagerness.

He pried the cover off with his fingers, Binnie poked the light
into it. "Books," said Ed, "that have been burned." He reached
in and took out a handful of paper, partly charred. It was bulky
stuff.

"It's part of a book all right!" said Binnie. "Part of the bind-
ing and some of the pages."

"Yup," said Ed softly, and reached in for more of it. "Sure
enough," he declared, "it's part of a book. No. Parts of several
books. Look—different type, different paper."

"Hold it steady," said Binnie. "Let's see what kind of books."

They read together part of a burned page: " . . . *recovers for
any damage he may have suffered down to the date of bringing his
action. But if the nuisance consists of a permanent structure, the
weight of authority in this . . . not only may but must recover pro-
spective damage also. . . .*"

"A law book!" said Binnie.

"Law book all right," Ed said. He had been kneeling beside the open hole, and now he sat back on his heels. "But why in hell?" He took out the rest of the contents of the can, laid everything carefully on the ground. "Bits of law books. But why? I don't get it."

"You don't get what?"

"Why it's burned. Why it's buried. What the devil does it mean? And why did this mess seem important to Dodo Brown? Why did somebody shoot him? On account of this junk?" He put the burned pages back into the can. "I don't get it." He put the cover on the can, picked it up and stood up. "Let's get out of here, Binnie. This thing not only puzzles me; it gives me the creeps."

He took the light from her and slowly searched the surrounding land with it. It was all blackness and stillness. "Let's go home," he said. He handed Binnie the light, picked up the shovel and they headed back to the car.

"I don't get it," he kept saying. "Why does anybody burn law books—law text books? Hilliard Wells or anybody else. Why? I don't get it. They have some significance. Dodo died because they have some significance. But what the devil is it?"

"If Dodo was smart enough to see that they had some significance," Binnie put in quietly, "why aren't we that smart?"

"Who knows?" Ed said with some irritation. "Maybe he buried things the way a dog buries a bone—just by instinct, whether they had significance or not."

"He got shot for burying them."

"Wait a minute," Ed corrected her. "He didn't get shot for burying them. He got shot for trying to take me to them."

"Which is pretty nearly one and the same thing."

"Maybe it is, maybe it isn't." They had reached the car. Ed opened the door and motioned Binnie in, got in himself, swung the car out into the road and back toward home. "I've got a funny feeling," he said, "as if this episode isn't over yet. I've got a feeling we're being watched and waited for."

"What do you mean, waited for?"

"I don't know. I can't explain it. I've just got the feeling."

The gray road sped back underneath them. "Are you going to take those burnt law books to Chief Tomlin?" Binnie asked.

"No," said Ed thoughtfully. "Not yet, anyhow. I'm going to take them home and try to dope them out. They mean something. I don't know what but maybe it'll dawn."

They came into the lighted portion of Proctor Street and turned into Walden. Ed took the driveway in a spurt. Mike was barking ferociously behind closed windows.

"I wonder what *that's* for," said Ed. He eased the car to a stop in the garage. "That dog's getting nerves."

They got out of the car, Ed took the tin can, and they walked onto the driveway.

"Now I've got the creeps," said Binnie. "And don't ask me why."

They came out of the shadow of the garage and into bright moonlight.

Ed heard the snapping of a twig off to the right, in the direction of the bushes in the yard. He turned his head quickly, put his finger on the button of the flashlight.

And then it happened.

He flung Binnie cruelly back against the wall of the garage and heard her cry out in pain. He had no time to dodge back himself.

There was the blaze of a gun, not twenty yards away. He heard three shots and the fourth got him.

He cried out involuntarily. The can tumbled out of his hands, he spun around the way Dodo Brown had spun, and he went down flat and hard on his face like a dead bird with wings outstretched.

17
DREAM AGAIN

I

It was the same dream and yet it wasn't the same dream. Somehow it had been edited, probably by the Editor to End All Editors: Sponsor Lattimer. To begin with, this time Ed was walking alone instead of with Walt. Where he was walking, Ed didn't know. Again it was down a street whose identity he could not determine. Again it seemed a little like Hollywood Boulevard, this time down near Grauman's Chinese, and then it did the same trick again and became something like Michigan Boulevard with a wind coming off the lake fit to blow your head off. He kept wishing the wind would blow his head off because it was a head that was no good to anyone; it was big as a block house and yet light as a meringue and it had an ache in it that was the granddaddy of all headaches. . . . Ed walked into the gigantic Polish wedding cake that was the Wrigley Building and down the long corridor toward Studio A. There was Harry Liebowitz, just as before, waiting at the entrance to the studio, washing his thin hands and saying something that again was obliterated by the howling of a loudspeaker in the wall, the loudspeaker bearing the label: "Mister Lattimer, the Sponsor." This time Mister Lattimer stuck his head out of the loudspeaker and accused Ed of something, but his voice was too loud for Ed to make out what he was saying. Ed went right on into Studio A and there was Walt Tuttle behind glass in the control booth giving merry hell to the cast of *Home Town* out there on the stage. Ed would have tipped his hat to the lady members of the cast but no one could reach up to the top of a head as big as that. The cast was standing up at the several microphones and Walt had his stop watch in his hand, and then suddenly he stopped giving them all merry hell and told them to stand by. The announcer, who had very big feet and very curly hair, stepped up to his mike and waited, and the orchestra leader tapped his stick and held it up for attention. "Thirty seconds," said Walt. "Now let's make it good. Don't forget: This is the last episode. This is where we catch the killer. With a hey-nonny-nonny!" "And a hotcha," said Ed. "Hey, Walt, look at my big head." But Walt paid no attention to him. The second hand on the studio clock crawled like the leg of a spider and stood straight up and Walt shot the go-ahead signal. The orchestra began to play the theme music. Walt faded it out with his right hand and with the other hand stabbed a finger at the announcer. It was the commercial, selling Lattimer's goods, so Ed made a superhuman effort and reached up as far as he could and put his fingers in his ears. "I don't have to listen to *this*," he said, and closed his eyes too. But it seemed he kept them closed too long, for when he opened them they were already in the show. It was a queer sort of script. It was that same damn parade again; no, not just the same. It was the little radio town of Stedham, but this time is was a parade of books. And not exactly a parade of books either. It was a parade of people carrying books. They were all so loaded up with books that you couldn't see who they were, for the books in their arms were piled up to the tops of their heads and they staggered along under the great weight of them. Ed was sitting on the low fence that ran around the post office lawn and Walt was sitting beside him. For a while they watched the parade and then Walt said quietly, without looking at Ed: "What happened to your head, Ed?" And Ed said, without looking at Walt: "A guy shot me." They watched the parade for a minute or two and then Walt asked: "What guy?" "The same guy that shot you," Ed replied. And they got up off the fence and followed the parade out of town to a big field and everybody in the parade began to dump the books in a heap, until the heap towered as high as a house. Then someone came running up with a torch and set fire to the heap and it blazed like the fires of hell on a windy afternoon. It was a very weird business. Everybody kept running around, having a good time, throwing more books on the fire. Then, without saying a word, Walt walked up to the fire, reached into it, took out some of the books and came back to where Ed was standing. "You know what those books are?" he asked. "Those are law books. Now who the devil would want to burn law books?" And he held out the charred remains and showed them to Ed.

II

Ed woke up with a start, in a cold sweat. Binnie was sitting beside him. It was daylight. "Hullo," she said. "How do you feel?" Her eyes were moist.

Ed licked parched lips. "I'm dizzy. I want a drink of water."

She gave him some, through a bent tube. "That's better. What day is it?"

"It's tomorrow, dear," she said. "It happened last night."

"Uh uh." He tried to think. "What happened?"

"Somebody shot you and got away."

"I remember. The stinker. Did you get hurt, kid?"

"No. I ran after him, but he got away."

Ed grinned. "*You* ran after him. What do you think *you* are, a posse?"

It was her turn to grin. "Well, not a very good one. They tell me I ran in the wrong direction."

"That's good. Just suppose you'd caught him. Hey!"

"What, Ed?"

"Am I hurt badly?"

"No." The tears welled up. "We're lucky. One bullet creased the side of your head. It isn't bad."

"Then why the hell am I so damn dizzy?"

"Well, in the first place, it wasn't a love pat, darling; it was a bullet. And in the second place, the doctor gave you some nembutal."

"Jeepers, I'll say he did. I'm going ring-around-the-rosie."

"You'd better shut your eyes and go to sleep again." He looked around him. He was in the spare room. "What am I?" he asked. "A guest?"

"It's all right," Binnie said. "They brought you here first and the doctor said not to move you. I'll be here. I'll sleep on the couch in the corner."

"Okay, Commissioner." He closed his eyes. Mike, who was at the foot of the bed, came up and licked his hand. Binnie leaned over and kissed Ed on the lips, then tiptoed out.

III

The jig was up and no mistake about that. The cop wasn't after him for speeding, because he wasn't speeding when the police car first swung out after him. They were looking for his number. He was a fool. He should have made some provision for changing the plates, but there was no time to think about that now.

He swore at the woman in the seat beside him, because she was weeping in a hysterical way that took his mind off his driving, and at eighty miles an hour, you needed to keep your mind on the driving.

"For God's sake, Anna, shut up!" he snapped at her. "You'll make me run this car off the road!"

"I don't care," Anna moaned. "I don't care. Now they'll catch us and then think what'll happen to me!"

"To *you*. Think what'll happen to *me!*"

She began to weep more vehemently than before.

"I want to go home," she kept saying over and over, as a child would say it through tears. "I want to go back to my husband. I want to go home."

He was at the end of his patience but he had a shred of chivalry left. "Look, Anna," he said. "When we make the next turn, I'm going to stop. Reach back and get your bag. Have it in your lap. Be ready to get out fast."

"But what'll I *do?*" she moaned.

"Do? It's easy for *you*. *Get the bag—you hear me!* You'll duck into the bushes. You'll wait till the police car has gone past. There's a bus due along here pretty soon. It'll take you back to Merrick and you can get another bus for Hamsted. You can be home before your husband gets suspicious."

"But where'll I tell him I was last night?" she wept.

"Use your head!" he snapped angrily. "You had a fight with him yesterday, didn't you? Tell him you got mad and went to stay with your aunt. You can cover yourself."

"I'm afraid!" she whined through her tears. "I'm afraid."

There was no time for more wards. The car shot around the next turn and he pumped the brakes till it came to a stop.

"Get out!"

"But what about you?" she wailed in sudden remorse.

"*Get out!*"

She flung open the door, got out quickly and ran down the roadside bank and into the thick bushes. The car was already on its way. She did not pause until she heard the police siren go screaming past and fade away down the road. Then she sat on her suitcase and began to cry again.

The police car was gaining. Three miles more and it closed the gap and ran the fugitive off the road and to a stop. The cops came out, ready for business.

"Get 'em up, brother!" Hilliard Wells put his hands up slowly. "Your name Wells—Hilliard Wells?" Wells nodded. "You're under arrest."

"What are the charges?"

"Plenty of charges. Assault with a dangerous weapon will do for one. Come on—get out. You can be a guest in our car."

IV

Johnnie Forsythe was at the wheel of the stolen car. Gregg was in back with the old man. Night had just come.

"For God's sake," Gregg pleaded, "find a doctor, Johnnie."

"How is he?"

"I think he's dying."

The old man lay stiff and twisted in Gregg's arms, his mouth open, his eyes wide and glazed and his breath coming hard.

"Hold on, Pa," Gregg kept saying over and over. "Hold on, Pa. We'll get you to a doc. We'll get you to a doc. Don't you be afraid, Pa."

Johnnie spotted a doctor's sign and jerked the wheel over and they jolted into the driveway. Johnnie bolted out of the car, ran across the lawn to the front door and stabbed at the bell. Then he ran back and helped Gregg get the old man out of the car. Together they carried him up on the front porch where a tall, bald-headed man with a quick eye waited in the light of the doorway.

'You the doc?" Gregg's teeth were chattering, and not from cold.

"Yes, bring him in. What's happened?"

"I dunno. I guess maybe it's a shock."

"Bring him in." He led the way into his office. "Put him on the couch."

The ministrations were brief. The old man lay still as death. The doctor led Johnnie and Gregg out of the office.

"Can't you do anything for him, Doc?" Johnnie begged. "Can't you bring him out of it?"

"I'm afraid not. There's nothing more we can do. We might get him to the hospital, but I'm afraid it would be too late."

The hard-boiled Gregg broke down and began to weep.

"Shut up!" said Johnnie. "You think that's going to do any good?"

A car drove up to the door. There was the sound of footsteps on the porch. The doorbell rang and the doctor answered it.

Two state troopers. "Sorry to bother you, Doctor. That's a stolen car out in your driveway. Do you know who brought it in?"

There was no fight left in Gregg or Johnnie, but the police never took the old man. He died as the doorbell rang.

V

Carl Benjamin, thief and embezzler, was arrested in a gambling raid in New York City. Within six hours he was on a train, in custody, and headed for Hamsted.

VI

Ed was sitting at a desk he didn't recognize, before a typewriter he had never seen before, and he was cracking out copy for a radio show that was somehow terribly confused with real life. He kept getting into the script himself, and then Walt got into it. It made sense and yet it didn't make sense. *I must be slipping*, he said, and he cried out for Walt.

But it wasn't Walt who came. It was Harry Liebowitz. Harry floated in from nowhere, with a batch of papers that looked as if he had snatched them out of the wind.

"Ed, in heaven's name," he shrieked, "you've got to help us out with this script! Where's Walt? Where the devil is Walt? I want some help with this script!"

Harry sprawled his papers out on the desk. "Look— for the love of Mike, Ed, look: We're stuck! Here we got a tragedy in the little town of Hamsted."

"Stedham," said Ed.

"Hamsted!" Harry screamed.

"Stedham," said Ed. "Hamsted is where I live. Stedham is the radio town."

"*So what!*" Harry shrieked. "What *difference* does it make? Stedham is only Hamsted backwards!"

"Sure," said Ed, getting mad and excited himself. "Just as Foss Leonard is Leonard Foss backwards! This is nuts! The whole thing is nuts! Everything is backwards! It's loony! Foss Leonard is backwards. Hamsted is backwards. *Everything* is backwards! Backwards! *Backwards! Backwards!*"

VII

Ed woke up in a cold sweat.

Everything was backwards! Sure! Of course! Everything was backwards—*everything!* That was it! That was the answer! That was the answer to the whole thing! That was why it had happened to Walt! Of course! Walt had hit it—Walt knew! That's why it had happened to Walt!

He sat up in bed.

It was dark in the room and it was dark outside. There was a spot of moonlight on the floor and he could make out Binnie's form on the couch in the corner. He could hear her breathing softly.

There was a hammer in his head and it bludgeoned him unmercifully. He poked his feet out of the covers and on to the floor.

Mustn't wake Binnie. The rug was warm but the floor was cold and his bandaged head was full of helium. He tiptoed out drunkenly. Mustn't wake Binnie. She wasn't coming this time—not this time.

There was a monster at his side as he went through the door. Mike. Mike licked his hand and followed silently.

He got to the master bedroom and, in the dark, found some clothes and his car keys. He pulled a pair of pants on over his pajamas, and a sweater, and almost fell on his face trying to put on his shoes. His coat was downstairs. Never mind a hat. No hat would fit on that head.

He tiptoed along the hall and down the stairs. There were so many noises in his head he couldn't tell whether he was walking silently or not, but anyway Binnie didn't stir.

He found his topcoat on the clothes tree. Getting into it was like wrestling with taffy, but he made it. Mike escorted him to the back door and licked his hand again. Ed went out, closed the door, managed the back stairs successfully and headed for the garage. There was a zest in the night air. It cleared away a little of the helium. He got into the car and drove off.

Ed was in front of a house, and he stood looking up at it as David looked up at Goliath. The master thought was clear enough in his mind; it was the details of the plan that eluded him. It seemed he had a plan; it must have been in that sudden, frigid, lucid moment when he wakened from his dream that the plan came, born whole and fully matured in that shocked in-stant; during an interval when nembutal and that dull throbbing pain in the head stood aside for just long enough.

And so he looked up at the house and held on to a telegraph post and did his best to collect whatever of his wits would be collected.

In a minute or two he had had enough.

He took what seemed like a painfully precarious route along the side of the house, and just before he came to the window that he intended to try, he fell on his face. He got to his feet with a difficulty and looked to see what he had fallen over. It was a long-handled sod cutter.

Just the thing. Carrying it, he went on to the window, reached up with the blade end of the cutter and tried the window. It was locked. He moved along to the next window. Unlocked. He slid it open quietly.

But the worst was yet to come. Even with a clear head and a body unencumbered with pain and fatigue and drugs, it would have been a struggle to get through that window. The sill was just above his reach. He couldn't jump for it because there wasn't a jump in him. In a strange kind of dull despair he trudged on along the side of the house until he found something on which he could stand—a galvanized iron pail which he carried back to the open window.

He set it down, bottom up, got up on it and nearly fell off. He rested for half a minute, hands holding onto the sill-like claws, and then when he had a little more strength, he began to haul himself inside.

It simply couldn't be done. There wasn't strength enough in him, and the pain in his head was so great that that alone would have been enough to keep him from doing it. And yet he did it, because his terrific rage at what was in that house boosted him straight through the window, so that he piled over the sill, fell face first on to the floor, all aheap, and lay there in an agony of pain and sweat and dizziness and nausea.

He lay there for nearly five minutes, panting and waiting for his strength to return. Then he got to his feet and reached into his topcoat pocket to see if the flashlight had been able to keep up with him. It had. He shot its light across the floor.

Dining room. Dining table, sideboard, china closet.

He turned off the light and stood listening. No sound except the busy little tick of a clock. He turned the light on again, crossed the dining room to the door, leaned against the door frame for several seconds, then went through.

Living room. Heavy cushioned chairs, a divan, coffee table, bookcases, a Governor Winthrop desk. He went first to the bookcases, scanned the books carefully. Then he turned to the desk.

It was not locked. As he opened it there rose the fragrance of Evening in Paris. A woman's desk. Probably nothing there. But he would look just the same. He sat down. He went through the pigeonholes and the drawers, above and below. Nothing.

He got up with an effort. His head, very large, seemed to rock from side to side, like a metronome. He had to stand very still for half a minute, holding onto the back of the chair. Then he set forth again.

He got out into the hall, where the staircase led upstairs. Again he put out the light and stood listening. This time there was no sound at all. . . .

He shot forth the light again, and crossed the hall to a door that stood ajar. He pushed the door open a little farther and went in, closing the door behind him. The light went like a yellow finger from object to object. Armchair. Bookcase. Cabinet. Couch. Desk, piled high with papers.

Again he went first to the bookcase, read each book title with eyes that throbbed with pain. Nothing there.

He went to the cabinet. It was not locked. He opened it. It contained pipes and tobacco, cigars, three bottles of liquor, a decanter of wine, matches, pipe cleaners, cigarettes. He studied the various items carefully, slowly. There didn't seem to be anything there.

Like a slow-motion picture, he went to the desk. Something in his head was going in slow circles: Maybe the whole head was going in slow circles; he didn't know. He sat down at the desk, put down the flashlight and held on to the edge of the desk with both hands. He had to concentrate very hard to remember what he was looking for. He wanted very much to go to sleep, then and there. He would have given every last cent he had to put his head down on the desk and get just ten winks. He was full of wounds and dope and sleep and pain and he was no good for the job he had set out to do.

But something told him he was too near the end to give up.

He paid little attention to the papers on the desk. He opened the center desk drawer, pushed back the chair and opened the drawer wide, began to sort over the articles inside. Pencils, pens, erasers, elastic bands, paper clips; papers, papers, papers. He took the papers out and looked them over one by one. No good. This was today. What he wanted was yesterday.

He closed the center drawer and opened the top drawer on the left. Odds and ends, a couple of small books, but no law books; a stapler, a box of staples. . . . The next drawer down: blank typewriter paper, some white, some yellow. Nothing there. The next drawer down: a cash record, personal bookkeeping; too recent, no good.

The drawers on the right: Top drawer. More pipes, more tobacco, a cigarette lighter. . . . Second drawer down. A few tools; a screwdriver, a small wrench, a tack hammer, a small metal box of nails. . . . The last, the bottom drawer. It was jammed and cluttered. This was the catch-all. Papers, books, clippings, carbon paper, a foot rule. He examined the papers, he examined the books and clippings. He was very sick and tired and discouraged and there was left only a small wooden box far back in the drawer. He took it out and set it in front of him on the desk and opened it. It was a very ordinary cigarette box, of flimsy maple, but it was not used for cigarettes. It was full of such foolish things as tarnished cuff links and dead collar buttons, bits of a broken gold chain, a couple of collar pins, a necktie pin, a very small pocketknife, pearl-handled, and a high school pin.

Only the high school pin quickened his pulse. He picked it up, held it eagerly in the light. "Cranshaw High School," it said in gold letters around the edge. The rest of the design he ignored. He fumbled with the pin, trying to turn it over. It was small and his fingers were thumbs and they were trembling with a tremendous excitement. The pin fell to the floor. He bent down, big head and all, and picked it up. He turned it over, to look at the back.

This was it! The end of the line. Finis. Curtain!

For there, scored deep in the back of the pin, long forgotten, were the initials "L. F."

His chair faced the opening door. There was a click and the light went on, and the two men stared at each other for ten seconds without moving.

Then Ed broke the silence. He held up the high school pin and said in a whimsical, almost foolish-sounding voice:

"Hello, Leonard Foss."

Quietly, Paul Hastings closed the door behind him. He looked pretty bad. He wore pajamas and slippers and a robe thrown over his shoulders. His left arm was still in a sling. In his right hand he had a gun. He was white-faced and unsteady, but his lips were a firm, hard gray line, and his eyes were alight with the light that glints off steel.

Ed still held up the high school pin. "L. F.," he said. "Leonard Foss. You forgot about this, Paul."

"You're a fool," said Hastings. "That's my wife's pin. Her name was Leora Franklin."

"Like hell," said Ed. "Look, Paul: I found some burned law books. A lawyer who was once a newspaper man wouldn't have to burn law books, but a newspaper man who was once a lawyer would have to burn 'em to keep us from knowing he was once a lawyer. You should have burned 'em years ago, Paul."

He got up. He moved around the desk, not away from Hastings but toward him. "You're crazy," said Hastings. "And you're a housebreaker. I'm going to give it to you, Ed. You're just a dead burglar tonight. Stay where you are."

"Sure," said Ed, and kept on coming. He put the pin in his pocket and walked in a slow straight line toward, Hastings. "Walt was smart, wasn't he, Paul? He doped you out and put you in a radio script. Nobody would recognize you but yourself, because it was all backwards, like Alice Through The Looking Glass. What was he doing—smoking you out, Paul, because he didn't have enough proof about Calla's murder? Was he forcing you to play the rest of your hand, Paul? You played it, didn't you? You killed him. You killed Walt and Burdick and Dodo to keep us from finding out you'd killed Calla. You did, didn't you, Paul?"

Hastings lifted the gun a little more and fired. Ed didn't feel anything, so he figured the shot must have missed him. He kept moving toward Hastings.

"You did, didn't you, Paul?"

There was an ugly little smile on Hastings' face as the gun went off a second time. This time it wasn't a miss. Ed felt a sharp pain in his arm, but it didn't stop him.

It wasn't like the dull, stupefying pain in his head. It was a pain that enraged him, that made him leap for Hastings. The gun clicked, clicked, clicked.

Ed had him by the throat. Hastings enveloped him, good arm and bad, and they went down on the floor with a terrific crash. They rolled over and over, fighting like two madmen, each wounded yet ignoring wounds.

Now Ed was on top and he still had Hastings by the throat and he sat on his chest and smashed Hastings' head against the floor. The door opened. Leora Hastings screamed. She ran to Ed, grabbed his coat, tried to tear him away, then beat him with her fists. But Ed was a determined leech and he hung on.

She ran to the telephone on the desk. She was calling the police, frantically.

"That's fine!" Ed gloated. "That's fine! That's just what we want! Go ahead and call 'em! Call 'em all!"

And he hung onto Paul Hastings' throat for all he was worth, allowing him only enough air to stay alive.

18

CONFESSION OF A MURDERER

I

My true name is Leonard Foss. The following statement I make of my own free will, without duress. I make this statement for two reasons: One, because I was to present the facts as they really are. There will be a great deal of distortion of facts before the matter is done, but at least there will be one true statement. The second reason is that my wife has asked me to tell the truth. If I am not guilty, she says, I must say I am not guilty even with my last breath. If I am guilty, I must say so now. She will stand by me no matter which declaration I make, so long as it is the truth. If I lie now, as I have lied for a long time, I shall lose her too, as I have lost everyone else: I am coward enough not to want to face these last things alone. Therefore I tell the truth.

Not that my confession is necessary for my conviction. The facts are as plain as the cards in a deck. When it became known that my true name was Leonard Foss and that I was formerly a lawyer, it was a simple matter to examine the alumni lists of the nation's law schools, find my name, then turn to the year book of my graduating class and find my photograph there. I have not changed considerably in appearance since then.

There is no question: I am Leonard Foss, disbarred lawyer; disbarred years ago in a jury bribing case whose details are of no importance now. I was guilty, I was disbarred. I became a newspaper man. I came to Hamsted, took over a bad newspaper and made a good one of it.

I met and fell in love with Calla Forsythe. Or perhaps I should say that she fell in love with me and that I took advantage of that love, for I would not marry her even when I knew that she was going to have a child, nor afterwards, when she had the child. I was ambitious and selfish. Such a marriage was not in my plans.

Calla kept after me to marry her, but she did not threaten to expose me until she learned that I was going to marry someone else. Then she did threaten me.

There seemed to be only one way out. I took her for a drive and a walk in the woods. I killed her the day before my marriage. The murder was blamed on a vagrant or vagrants unknown.

Only one person had any vestige of suspicion: Jacob Burdick. It was no more than a suspicion. Calla had never told him the name of the father of her child, but he did know what few people knew, that she had a child. And he had his suspicions. But he had no proof.

When Calla died, Burdick communicated with Walter Tuttle, and when Tuttle came to Hamsted he set about to confirm Burdick's suspicion. He hired a private detective to investigate my past. The detective learned that I had once been a lawyer, that my true name was Leonard Foss. I know this to be a fact because the same private detective, for the modest sum of five hundred dollars, informed me of exactly what Tuttle had done and what he had learned. So I was forewarned.

So Tuttle had my true name and the story of my past, but these facts were hardly enough to justify an indictment for murder. However, he could scheme to drive me into the open; he could try to make me betray myself. The method: the radio show. He wrote the story of Calla's death in such a way as to point out to me, and only to me, that he knew I was the man in Calla's life and in her death. He did this by a series of reversals. The villain of the piece was Foss Leonard, instead of Leonard Foss; the town was Stedham instead of Hamsted. Calla was Lily Newcomb. Foss Leonard was a lawyer who had once been a newspaper man instead of vice versa. It was a clever device, but it could lead to only one thing: I was not sure just how much Tuttle knew, so I went to the store that night and asked questions. Tuttle shot his bolt prematurely, accused me point-blank. I put a bullet through him.

The Brewer's Blend tobacco that Oscar Batchelder had seen in the store that night was Jacob Burdick's. Of course Burdick was not present when I shot Tuttle, but I needed no tobacco clue to tell me that he had worked with Tuttle. Tuttle's double-crossing detective had included that information in the five hundred dollars worth. And so I set out to get Burdick.

Burdick was elusive but I was persistent, and I had good luck when I saw Burdick give the first note to the Halleck boy who delivered it to MacIntyre while I followed in my car. It was then that I tried to kill Burdick the first time.

I drove at once toward Burdick's place, but on the way I spotted him heading for his rendezvous with MacIntyre. I left my car, followed him on foot and tried to shoot him. He got away in the darkness.

The second note was delivered to MacIntyre in the cemetery during the burial of Walter Tuttle. It required no great stretch of imagination to figure out that this note was also from Burdick. That night, I trapped Burdick in his shack, shot him and buried him where he was found. Before he died I forced him to tell me about his rendezvous with MacIntyre. I went to that place and tried to kill MacIntyre by running him down, but I failed.

My greatest strength, of course, was in the position of confidence that I held. I was trusted by the police, I was trusted by Ed MacIntyre. (Not even Tuttle's coauthor knew of his suspicions!) MacIntyre became, little by little, more dangerous than the police. I tried to mislead him. When I discovered Carl Benjamin stealing at the drug store, I tried to identify him as the murderer. But that didn't go in very deep.

Immediately after, however, opportunity presented itself. MacIntyre's private detective discovered that lawyer Hilliard Wells had a past. The detective, MacIntyre and I went to face Wells. Wells brazened it out and we left, without satisfaction for the moment. I, however, returned within a few minutes with the purpose in mind of making Wells try a getaway, which would strengthen suspicion against him.

Wells had not admitted to MacIntyre and the detective that he was the man they accused him of being, one Harry Wellman of Toledo. I forced his hand by attempting to put through a telephone call to the wife he had deserted years before. Wells stopped me with a bullet—and ran away.

Again circumstances played into my hands. Wells' shot gave me what looked like a perfect alibi. I was badly wounded, and perhaps moving would do me serious harm, but I had to risk it. I was convinced that MacIntyre must be put out of the way. If I could do it and return to Wells' office and pretend I had never left it. . . .

It was dark. The streets were empty. I got downstairs and into my car. I was bleeding but not too profusely. (I left no trail of blood anywhere except in my car, where it was discovered only after I was arrested and jailed.) I drove to MacIntyre's street and tried to plan my next move. A shot through the window seemed the best plan. I got out of the car and walked as far as the bushes that stand beside the couch, when the dog heard me and began to bark. I might have been discovered then, but again I was lucky. A few moments later, Lawyer Absalom Reynolds came up the path. His visit was brief and violent. He warned MacIntyre to stop investigating his personal life and he left at once, without even stepping inside the door. When he left, I was able to get out of the bushes and on to the porch. The dog began to bark again. Immediately, someone else arrived. It was Dodo Brown this time. He went inside. But the dog knew that there was still someone outside. He began to bark viciously again. MacIntyre locked him up.

I saw and heard the rest of it through a window. And as I watched and listened, I began slowly to realize what I had not realized before: that in the foolishness, the idiocy of Dodo Brown there was a core of the most damaging shrewdness, an uncanny knack for putting a finger on the significant. It was he who had brought to light the body of Calla's child. It was he who now was about to bring to light a danger even closer to me. I had many years before destroyed everything that could conceivably connect me with the past. I did not believe that I was foolhardy in keeping a few law books—until it became clear to me that Ed MacIntyre was puzzling over the significance of his own radio script with respect to the real-life story that was having its run in our town of Hamsted. Would he sooner or later see the reversals Tuttle had made use of—would he see enough to point to me? I couldn't risk it. I burned the books in my yard, in the incinerator barrel, and at night carried the contents of the barrel to the town dump, where I scattered them. I thought I had been seen by no one. I was wrong. I was seen by Dodo Brown. And now Dodo Brown was about to bring his find to the attention of Ed MacIntyre. To prevent this I followed them in my car and shot the boy.

I returned then to Hilliard Wells' office, where I was found with a complete alibi, under such circumstances as should have convinced anyone that I could not have murdered Brown. They took me home. I insisted that it be home and not to a hospital: I might have to get out again.

It became apparent at once that I must get out again. I was weak from the bullet wound and from my mission to kill Dodo Brown, but when MacIntyre told me of his plan to go looking again that very night for the burned book remnants, I knew that I must write finis to him too. When the doctor gave me a sleeping capsule, I only pretended to swallow it and shortly after I pretended to be in deep sleep. When my wife went to her room, I got out of the house. My car was still in front of Hilliard Wells' office, but my wife's car was in the garage. The garage is on the north side of the house; my wife's bedroom is on the south; she did not hear me leave.

I waited in ambush for MacIntyre at his home. I tried to kill them both, MacIntyre and his wife. I failed.

That was the beginning of the end. The true significance of the radio script, which he was bound to see sooner or later, he saw now, suddenly. He came to my house, searching for a final clue to substantiate his theory. He found it—something I had overlooked—a high school pin bearing the initials "L. F." That was the end. The murderer was not a lawyer who had once been a newspaper man, but a newspaper man who had once been a lawyer; a man whose name had once been Leonard Foss and who had forgotten to destroy so harmless a thing as a high school pin.

So this is the confession of Leonard Foss. I make no excuse for anything I have done. I have killed four people with premeditation. I ask no mercy. I ask nothing except that my wife stand with me until the end. This she will do. The rest of the world does not matter. . . .

II

Hicks and Wasserman were the two radio writers. They were dying a slow death at two hundred and fifty dollars a week, strictly on a make-good-week-to-week basis, no options. They were getting daily injections of the Slade Lattimer Sponsor Poison. Hicks, who had never been to Hollywood, had Hollywood stomach; Wasserman, who had been to Hollywood and back, had Hollywood stomach, claustrophobia, and was only a ten-cent ride from a nervous breakdown.

At the present moment they were in a huddle with Ed MacIntyre in the Hamsted Pharmacy. It was after hours. Harry Liebowitz was the anxious sheepdog herding his two lambs. Binnie was the soda jerk; she made cokes for them until she lost count.

They sat in the booth in front of the one in which Walt had been killed. Ed faced Hicks and Wasserman. Harry Liebowitz paced the floor, pausing to prompt them,

The opening speech had been made by Harry Liebowitz.

"Look, boys—you know what we want; you know what Mr. Lattimer wants. You know what we're gonna do. We're gonna take advantage of the nationwide publicity *Home Town* is getting because of the tie-up here. We're gonna revamp the script so as to make it as true to the real facts as possible at this stage of the game. We're gonna call spades spades and leave out only what the network boys make us leave out. You get it? This is the real thing: *Home Town* comes true! This is the most super-colossal humdinger of a baby that ever came down the creek and we're gonna do it up good and brown. It's gonna be as is, real life, red hot—"

"Only one thing, please," Ed interrupted quietly. "There were four murders. There are going to be several more if I am mentioned or my wife is mentioned or any reference is made to Walt."

"But for the love of cryin' out loud!" Harry protested. "What do you *mean?* We *got* to make reference!"

"You heard me, Harry."

Harry turned pleading hands to Binnie. "Binnie, for cryin' out loud, what is this? Can you make this guy listen to sense?"

"You want me to get murdered too?" Binnie inquired patiently.

"Oh, for Pete's sake!" Harry moaned. "We're licked before we start. We might as well pack up and go."

"Okay," said Ed, getting up. "Let's pack up and go."

"No-no-NO!" Harry shrieked. "Wait a minute! Can't you take a little literary exaggeration? All right, okay, so we can't make reference to Walt or you or Binnie. So we'll figure a way to get around it."

"And you submit all scripts to us for final approval," Binnie put in quietly. Ed looked up at her admiringly. "After," continued Binnie, "*after* Mr. Slade Lattimer gives *his* final approval."

Harry put out a helpless hand. "Now wait a minute, Binnie," he said softly. "Don't *do* this to me. Sponsors don't let *anybody* have a final approval after *theirs*. You *know* that! Ed, it ain't *done*."

"There's a first time for everything," Ed replied.

"And we'll take it in writing," said Binnie.

"But do you realize what you're *doing* to me? If I promise anything like that in writing, Lattimer will cut me in little pieces!"

"Look," Ed interrupted quietly but savagely, leaning across the table and looking at Harry. "*I've* already been cut in little pieces. I've been cut in little pieces and I've got a bullet crease in my dome, and most of the time my head still aches like something I don't know the word for. And Walt was my best friend and he was murdered. If you want any help from me, you're not going to make a hullabaloo about Walt. I don't want any pay for what I'm giving you, but you're going to do as I say."

"But we'll *glorify* Walt!" Harry pointed out, while Hicks and Wasserman nodded emphatically. "We'll make him a great hero, the man who is really responsible for the solving of the mystery. We won't do his memory any *harm!*"

"Put it in writing that I have final approval of all scripts. Put it in writing right now."

Harry was near tears. "All right," he said, reaching for a piece of paper and a pen. "All right. But Lattimer will murder me for this."

Two hours later, Ed threw up his hands. "Look," he said. "You don't get it. I can tell by your questions you don't get it. You aren't set to treat this thing the way it ought to be treated. Harry, look."

"Yes?" said Harry meekly, holding his breath and keeping fingers crossed.

"No offense, fellers," Ed said to Hicks and Wasserman, "but I'm going to do this script myself. It's got to be done the way Walt would want it done and I think I'm the only one who knows how he'd want it done, and I can't seem to get it over to you. That's my fault, so if you don't mind, I'll do the script myself. Not for pay, mind you. That's yours; you can have it."

Hicks and Wasserman did a good job of looking crestfallen. They were not as dumb as they looked, nor as dumb as Slade Lattimer thought they were. They had played their cards as Harry Liebowitz had coached them to do. They would remain on salary and get a bonus besides.

"I'll do the script only to the end of the Lily Newcomb story," Ed said. "From then on it's yours."

"Okay," said Harry, washing his hands eagerly. "Anything you say, Ed. Anything at all."

And he smiled broadly.

COACHWHIP PUBLICATIONS
CoachwhipBooks.com

COACHWHIP PUBLICATIONS
CoachwhipBooks.com

DEATH SAILS
THE NILE

F. Burks McKinley

COACHWHIP PUBLICATIONS
CoachwhipBooks.com

MURDER TAKES
THE VEIL

MURDER AT
ST. DENNIS

SISTER SIMON'S
MURDER CASE

THE MARGARET ANN HUBBARD
MYSTERY OMNIBUS

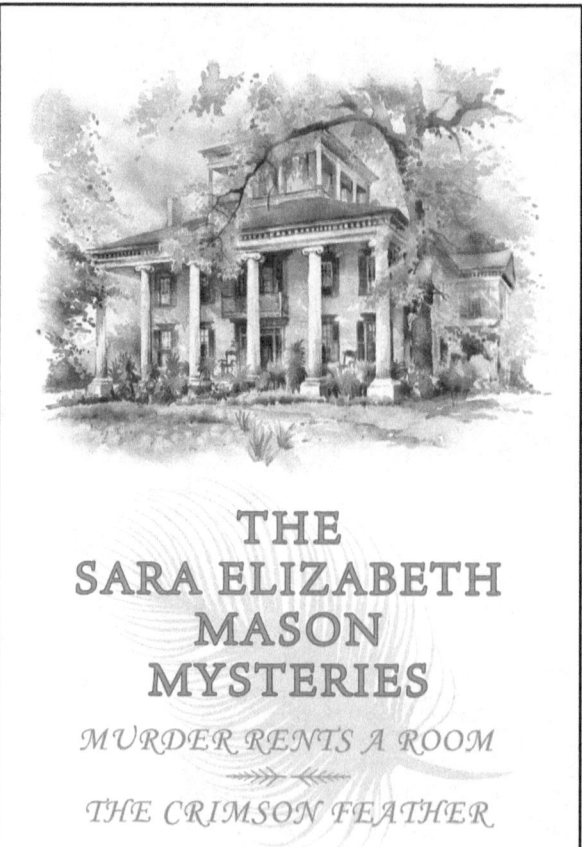

THE
SARA ELIZABETH
MASON
MYSTERIES

MURDER RENTS A ROOM

THE CRIMSON FEATHER

COACHWHIP PUBLICATIONS
CoachwhipBooks.com

THE
SARA ELIZABETH
MASON
MYSTERIES

THE HOUSE THAT HATE BUILT

>>>> <<<<

THE WHIP

COACHWHIP PUBLICATIONS
COACHWHIPBOOKS.COM

THE GOLDFISH
MURDERS

WILL MITCHELL

COACHWHIP PUBLICATIONS
CoachwhipBooks.com